Michael Underwood and The Murder Room

>>> This title is part of The Murder Room, our series dedicated to making available out-of-print or hard-to-find titles by classic crime writers.

Crime fiction has always held up a mirror to society. The Victorians were fascinated by sensational murder and the emerging science of detection; now we are obsessed with the forensic detail of violent death. And no other genre has so captivated and enthralled readers.

Vast troves of classic crime writing have for a long time been unavailable to all but the most dedicated frequenters of second-hand bookshops. The advent of digital publishing means that we are now able to bring you the backlists of a huge range of titles by classic and contemporary crime writers, some of which have been out of print for decades.

From the genteel amateur private eyes of the Golden Age and the femmes fatales of pulp fiction, to the morally ambiguous hard-boiled detectives of mid twentieth-century America and their descendants who walk our twenty-first century streets, The Murder Room has it all. >>>

The Murder Room
Where Criminal Minds Meet

themurderroom.com

Michael Underwood (1916–1992)
Michael Underwood (the pseudonym of John Michael Evelyn) was born in Worthing, Sussex and educated at Christ Church College, Oxford. He was called to the Bar in 1939 and served in the British army during World War Two. He returned to work in the Department of Public Prosecutions until his retirement in 1976, and wrote almost 50 crime novels informed by his career in the law. His five series characters include Sergeant Nick Atwell and lawyer Rosa Epton, of whom is was said by the *Washington Post* that she 'outdoes Perry Mason'.

The Man Who Killed Too Soon

Michael Underwood

An Orion book

Copyright © Isobel Mackenzie 1968

The right of Michael Underwood to be identified as the author of this work has been asserted in accordance with the Copyright, Designs and Patents Act 1988.

This edition published by
The Orion Publishing Group Ltd
Orion House
5 Upper St Martin's Lane
London WC2H 9EA

An Hachette UK company
A CIP catalogue record for this book is available from the British Library

ISBN 978 1 4719 0824 8

www.orionbooks.co.uk

To Simon Virgo

1

Richard Monk sat gazing out of the bus window at the seemingly endless vista of ramshackle suburban Tokyo. The towering complexes of steel and glass which dot the city's inner bounds were left behind and now they were ploughing through a grey sea of one-storey wooden houses and shops which covered the landscape like lumpy porridge as far as the eye could see. And everywhere there were people. Clean, neat, polite, teeming people. The most vivid impression he would take away from Japan would be of people in well-behaved masses, filling the pavements, swarming out of subway stations, surging round shrines. People – people who, despite the ant-hill conditions under which so many of them lived, managed to retain a natural dignity and respect for one another.

"And now we leave Tokyo and enter Yokohama," announced the guide in carefully articulated English. He was given to significant pauses in his utterances, but Richard had decided these were no more than the mental preparation required for his next foray into the English language. He was an elderly man in a battered panama hat, and resembled a schoolmaster who had throughout his life come off second best in the classroom's battles. Despite his announcement, the view outside remained the same. He might just as well have said "We've left the Atlantic and entered the Pacific."

Richard turned his attention to his fellow passengers. There were only thirteen of them, and a glance at the coloured ribbons attached to their lapel badges told him that not all of them were making the same tour as himself. Some would be returning to Tokyo in the evening. He counted only five green ribbons in addition to his own, who would be going on to Kyoto after a night in the shadow of Mount Fuji. One of the many things which had impressed him since his arrival in the country two weeks before was the quietly expert way the Japan Travel Bureau staff managed to shepherd its daily flocks of tourists, many of whom, though possibly as stupid as sheep, were far less amenable.

1

The front two rows were occupied by a party of six Americans and their cameras. They consisted of two middle-aged women, three teenage girls and a cheerful young man. Richard tuned in to their conversation and soon gathered that the women were sisters and the three girls their children, though he was unable to achieve a further break-down. The young man who had a crew-cut and traces of retreating acne was a soldier on leave from Korea. It appeared that he'd met up with one of the girls only the previous day, the one beside whom he was now sitting to their apparent mutual gratification. From time to time one of the other women would throw a small, doubtful frown in their direction, but otherwise she and her sister were absorbed in an interminable discussion about the way someone called Abby had recently refurnished her home. Richard gathered that the living-room was passable but that she had made a hideous hash of the main bedroom.

Behind this sextet sat two men whose language he identified after a time as French-Canadian. They spoke infrequently and then only with set, stony expressions so that he wondered why they bothered to communicate at all. On the opposite side of the aisle was an Indian couple who spoke in soft whispers and behind them a girl who, he later learnt, was Swedish and next to her a young man.

From where he sat, Richard was able to observe the whole scene without himself being observed – at least not without anyone actually turning round and staring blatantly at him. The price of this commanding position was to sit over the wheels, as he had discovered soon after departure.

The person who most attracted his attention was the young man sitting next to the Swedish girl. Richard reckoned him to be a year or two younger than himself, say twenty-nine or thirty. He was about six feet tall, well-proportioned and good looking despite a certain tendency to fleshiness about the face. He was listening with an abstracted air to something the Swedish girl was saying. His smile seemed to come on and off as though it was lit by neon. It had rather the same meaningless quality of neon, too.

This was the third occasion on which they had taken the same tour. The first had been ten days ago when Richard had become suddenly aware that he was being studied with inquisitive interest while their guide was diligently pointing out places of interest from the observation platform of Tokyo Tower. Then a few days later the young man had been on the same day trip to Nikko. Richard might not have paid him particular attention had he not again found himself the object of scrutiny on and off throughout the day. Once when he had deliberately intercepted a long, disconcerting stare, he had been accorded a quick, hopeful smile to which he had responded with a distant — and, he hoped, unambiguous — flicker.

As he now took his own time in a covert study of the young man, he tried to remember at which of the pick-up hotels in Tokyo he had joined the bus. He recalled that it was a new one near Shiba Park. English was his spoken language, that much Richard had gathered, though he had not yet been able to identify his country of origin. He certainly wasn't American or Canadian, but that still left a wide range of other possibilities.

While he was vaguely trying to establish his provenance from a casual examination of his profile, the young man suddenly turned and threw him a quick look over his left shoulder, as if to reassure himself that Richard was still on board the bus.

Richard returned his own attention to the scene outside. They had finally emerged from the built-up area and were travelling through a green landscape of knoll-like hills. Men and women in wide-brimmed straw hats were bent double planting in the paddy fields which stretched in neat, geometric patterns wherever the ground was flat. It all looked somehow removed from reality, like an elaborately dressed toyshop window.

Shortly afterwards the bus left the main road and a mile or two farther on turned into a car park.

"And now," said the guide with a hopeful smile, "we visit the awesome bronze Buddha of Kamakuro."

Richard waited until everyone else had got out before leaving his own seat and following the guide, who was holding aloft a small, fluttering blue flag as a rallying point for his flock. As he came up behind the two American women, he lingered long enough to discover that Abby's current husband was now under discussion. One of them thought he was cute, to which the other retorted that he might be cute, but he was still a little stinker.

Overtaking them, Richard made his own way up to the vast Buddha which gave the absurd impression of having outgrown its surroundings. The lips were curled in an air of superior disdain, but he was intrigued by the fastidiously folded hands with the thumbs and forefingers just touching as though the Buddha was telling a story which required the illustration of this delicate gesture.

Parties of cheerful, well-behaved schoolchildren swarmed everywhere, the girls in their sailor-suit uniforms, the boys in peaked caps and buttoned tunics. To Richard, these carefully marshalled hordes of children, with whom the parties of foreign tourists always became inextricably mingled at every sight-seeing Mecca, were as much a part of the teeming scene as Tokyo's rush-hour commuters.

As he turned away from the Buddha, a giggling schoolgirl thrust a camera into his hands and he obligingly snapped her and her grinning friend as they posed with arms round one another's waists. He returned the camera and exchanged bows with the two girls.

After leaving Kamakura they drove along the shoreline and gazed out at the rather turgid waters of the Pacific. Richard's thoughts turned idly to home. His flat in Mayfair and office in Bedford Square seemed even further than twelve thousand miles away,

For the last three years he had been head and sole principal of the firm of Richard Monk and Co., Solicitors, a position made the more enviable, in the general view, by the agreeable addition of an inherited fortune of £400,000. This not only enabled him to pick and choose his clients, but also to satisfy his nagging wanderlust by taking the sort of holidays that most could only dream about. Defending people in trouble, however, was a constant and salutary reminder that it needed little more than a sharp twist of fate for roles to become reversed.

The sight of a man fishing off the end of a small jetty made him think of Alan Scarby—Alan who was a barrister and his oldest friend, and who would fish in a water butt if there were nowhere else. When he got back to Tokyo he would have to give thought to presents for the Scarbys. Perhaps a camera for Alan, something uniquely Japanese and feminine for Jane, and for Sophie . . . Well, at two Sophie, who also happened to be his godchild, wasn't fussy about her presents.

The bus turned inland toward the mountains which were crested with creamy rolls of menacing cloud. During the next hour's drive, a girl, whose sole function seemed to be to open and close the door of the bus and count heads before they drove on again, sang to them. The songs all sounded exactly alike to Richard, though their subjects, as introduced by the guide, could hardly have been more varied.

Up in the mountains, the cloud appeared less menacing, though it successfully obscured all the surrounding peaks. Richard, who had grown up under the cosily vague impression that Mount Fuji could virtually be seen from one end of Japan to the other, felt severely disillusioned on finding it obliterated from view at only a few miles distance.

Lunch was taken at a hotel beside Lake Hakone. Richard entered the dining-room after the others and went over to sit at the same table as the Indian couple, pretending not to notice the silent invitation flashed him by the young man to join the Swedish girl and himself.

After the meal came a trip by steamer to the other end of the lake where their bus was waiting for them. A short drive brought them to a fantastic sight, a whole mountainside throbbing with the shrieking hiss of escaping jets of steam and a pervasive smell of sulphur hanging over everything.

It occurred to Richard as he moved along one of the paths to get a better camera shot that nature could outdo man any day in provision of the awe-inspiring. This was an alfresco hell's kitchen, and the appearance of the devil himself would not have come amiss.

He had strayed some distance from the rest of his party when he heard footsteps behind him, and turned his head to find the young man from the bus blocking the path.

"You're Mr. Monk, the London solicitor, aren't you?" Before Richard could say anything, he went on urgently, "My name's Eddie Butcher. I'm in dead trouble, Mr Monk. Will you help me?"

2

Whatever thoughts Richard Monk had been having about the young man who now introduced himself, acquiring him as a client on a Japanese volcanic mountainside had not been amongst them. For several seconds he just gazed at Butcher with an expression of quizzical disbelief as he tried to make up his mind how to reply to this wildly incongruous cri de coeur.

"How do you know my name?" he asked in a puzzled tone.

"I thought I recognised you that morning up Tokyo Tower. And then on the trip to Nikko, I was absolutely certain it was you. Anyway, I'd heard you tell the guide which your hotel was, so I just phoned up and asked if they had a Mr Monk staying and when they said they had I knew I'd been right."

"But that still doesn't explain how you recognised me in the first place?"

"Oh, from a photograph I'd once seen of you in a newspaper back home," he replied nonchantly.

"You sound like some photographic memory man."

For a moment Butcher himself looked puzzled, then his face broke into an engaging grin. "Now I get you! No, I don't remember everyone's picture, only those of people I might be able to get a bit of help from." His grin broadened. "Good defending lawyers are high on my list, however."

"I've been paid some funny compliments in some funny places," Richard remarked wryly, "but that one wins the jackpot."

"You will help me then?" Butcher said eagerly.

"How can I say? I don't know anything about you! I don't know what sort of help you require! Maybe it's a Japanese lawyer you should consult? You do realise that I have absolutely no professional status in this country?"

Butcher listened to him quietly, and when he had finished speaking said, "Ever heard of Casper? Ralph Casper?"

Richard gave a wary nod.

"I thought you might have." Butcher's expression became strained. In a grim tone he went on, "Well, I'm a fugitive

6

from Casper's justice."

Richard was suddenly aware of a new sound against that of hissing steam. He glanced down the path and saw their guide waving his small flag at them and calling out their names, at the same time pointing at the bus.

"We'd better run." He set off at a brisk pace with Butcher on his heels. "I gather from your ribbon that you're also on the trip to Kyoto?"

Butcher nodded, though Richard was only later to learn that this was no coincidence. As they climbed back into the bus, one of the American women said amiably, "We thought you'd gotten yourselves a hot bath."

"It's not my night for one," Richard replied with a smile.

Half an hour later they arrived at the hotel where they were to spend the night. It was a low, rambling building, the shape of a stretched-out Z, set half-way down a steep, thickly wooded mountainside. It had something of a hunting lodge atmosphere inside, with innumerable views of Fuji on the walls. This, Richard presumed, was to compensate for the coyly obscured real thing.

As he was signing the hotel register, Butcher came up beside him. "Can we have dinner together tonight?"

"All right."

"Shall I meet you in the bar at six?"

Richard looked at his watch and saw that it showed half past four. That gave him an hour and a half to unpack his pyjamas and toothbrush, have a bath—and do some thinking. He nodded. "Yes, that'll suit me."

As he lay in a piping bath whose water, a proud notice on the wall informed him, came direct from a natural hot spring, he tried to recall all he had heard about Casper. The problem always was with such people to know where fact ended and rumour took over. However, he had no reason to doubt the commonly held police view that he was Britain's most successful, sophisticated and ruthless gang-leader. His name was invariably linked by whispers with every major crime which had the acquisition of wealth by crooked means as its motive, though oddly enough it had never been suggested that he had anything to do with the Great Train Robbery. A crime reporter had once told Richard that he reckoned Caspar to be a millionaire as a result of his criminal enterprises, and his style of living, from all accounts, though surprisingly unostentatious, was in keeping with a bank balance which would have

7

made even a computer blink.

The nearest Richard himself had come to having anything to do with him was a couple of years before, when he had defended a man who had been charged with knifing one of Caspar's gang in a public-house brawl, and who was plainly far more scared of Caspar's retribution than he was of the judge's sentence. And yet the same crime reporter had told him that, to meet, Caspar was just like a top business executive—which, of course, in one sense he was.

One established basic fact about him was that the police had never come anywhere near putting him behind prison bars, and this was certainly not for want of trying. Indeed, Richard had understood from a senior Fraud Squad officer that they prowled ceaselessly round the perimeter of his empire looking for cracks, but the unhappy fact was that Caspar was held in considerably greater fear than were the police, a situation summed up by one of his henchmen who was alleged to have intimidated a witness on one occasion by saying, "We can kill you, the police can't."

When Richard entered the bar, Butcher was already there. He had changed and was wearing a pair of narrow fawn trousers and a blue cashmere jacket with silver buttons. On his feet were a pair of light suede shoes.

He waved a hand at the rows of bottles as Richard joined him. "What'll you have, Mr Monk? They've got the lot here, though I don't guarantee it's what the label says in every case. I had something in a Tokyo night club that was called French brandy and it tasted bloody awful. I reckon it was dregs from the Imperial moat."

"What's that you're drinking? Saké?"

"Yes. I don't like it when they serve it the temperature of armpits, but cold it's fine. I've grown quite a thirst for it. Will you join me?"

"No. I'll just have a beer."

"Japanese beer is not bad either."

They carried their drinks across to a table and sat down. There were only one other couple in the bar and they were in the far corner.

"How long have you been in Japan?" Richard asked, by way of opening the conversation.

"About three weeks. A bit over that. I left England two months ago and stopped off at a few places on my way here, like Beirut and Singapore and Australia and Hong Kong." He drained his glass and with a thoughtful expression sucked his lips. "Mind if I get a refill? Then I'll be ready to begin."

Richard watched him walk over to the bar. He moved easily, and reinforced the impression Richard had already gained of someone who could look after himself in most situations, even as a defecting member of Caspar's gang. When he returned to the table, he pulled out a packet of cigarettes and lit one after Richard had refused. He inhaled deeply and then let the smoke dribble from his nostrils and the corner of his mouth.

"As I told you this afternoon, Mr. Monk, I'm in dead trouble. Just how dead I've only realised this week. But I'm pretty sure that Caspar has found out I'm in Japan and that means I'm in real danger." He looked straight into Richard's face. "That's not being dramatic. It's a fact. The only thing is I don't want to end my days in a perishing foreign country. A fortnight on the Costa Brava is one thing: rotting on the other side of the world is another. I realise that now, even if I didn't two months ago." He took a gulp of his drink. "Also I'm homesick, Mr. Monk, and that's the truth. I want to go back to England whatever the risks and that's where you come in."

"Look, I suggest you start at the beginning and tell me why you left England in the first place. When I've heard the whole story, I'll tell you whether or not I can help you."

"Fair enough. I'll start earlier than that. My full name is Edmund Stephen Butcher; I'm twenty-eight years old and I was born in Reading. My father was a long-distance lorry driver. One day he drove away and never came back. I was nine at the time and I missed him bad. Soon afterwards someone called Uncle Bill moved in, and in due course he and my mother got married, but not before she'd had a couple of kids by him. Anyway, I never did care for Uncle Bill, so when I was fifteen I left home one fine morning and hitched a lift to London." He gave Richard an impish smile. "And I've been there ever since gravitating from one thing to another."

Richard decided that interesting listening though this part of Butcher's life might make, he would nevertheless guide him up to the present.

"When was it you met up with Caspar?"

"Nearly three years ago. Through Tony Tendo. He's one of Caspar's boys. Incidentally, if you're thinking Tendo and me met inside, you're wrong. In fact, I'll tell you now, I've never been to prison. Not prison proper that is. Just a spell in Borstal. Anyway, getting back to Tony Tendo and how I met him. I

9

was running a nice little racket at the time to do with home-wave sets and the money was absolutely pouring in. At the height of things I was getting as much as four hundred quid a day in fifteen shilling postal orders."

"What were your customers getting in return?" Richard inquired with wry interest.

"A few really did receive sets. Not bad they were either. But most of them got notices saying that due to popular demand there was bound to be some delay *et cetera*. Anyway, just as I was about to clear out for good with my suitcase of postal orders, Tendo turns up in the office I was renting." He broke off. "Do you know him by any chance?"

"As far as I know I've never heard of him."

"He's about six feet tall and four feet broad and has more muscle than a pack of gorillas. Anyway, the upshot was that he said he thought Caspar would be interested in meeting me. When he first began asking questions I reckoned he'd come along to get himself a hunk of my business and I don't mind telling you I was pretty relieved when no such thing was even suggested. Two days later we met at a pub in Southwark and he told me that Caspar would definitely like to meet me and that he'd drive me to his home as soon as we'd finished our drinks."

"Did you know anything about Caspar at this time?" Richard asked.

"Sure I knew about him. Like you know about the Attorney-General in your line of business. Though, mind you, Caspar wasn't as powerful then as he is now. There were other competitors in the field whom he's since taken over. Just as he took me over, because that's what happened. At that time he had a house out at Barnet—ruddy great place it was behind a high wall. Mind you, his present place near Weybridge is no smaller and if anything the wall's a bit higher.

"Well, we finish our beers and get into Tony Tendo's white Zodiac and drive out to Barnet. We go into a sort of study, the size of the Old Bailey, and there's Caspar sitting in front of a log fire reading *Country Life*—I always remember it was *Country Life*— just like he was deciding which grouse moor to rent next. Anyway, he says how he's heard I'm quite a smart boy and maybe I'd like to work for him. And I ask him what sort of work he has in mind, and he says running smart businesses just like I'd been doing but on a bigger scale, with bigger profits. He then tells me that if I agree, he can guarantee that

I'll be a rich man in far less time than I will be if I continue on my own. And I say supposing I don't agree, and Tony Tendo sort of stirs over on his chair in the corner and then I agree. And Caspar says he's sure I've made the wise decision as the day of the lone operator is over and he'd not like to have seen my business snatched from under my nose as would surely have happened." Butcher gave a grunt. "And nobody knew the truth of that better than Ralph Caspar." He fell into a meditative silence.

"And so?" Richard put in.

"And so I became a fully signed-up member of the Caspar gang. Over the course of the past three years I've run five phoney businesses for him. By 'for him' I mean that he was the principal shareholder and beneficiary."

"Were these what the law calls *long firm frauds?* That is, the acquisition of goods on credit by a bogus company and then their rapid sale below price before the company in question vanishes like a vapour trail?"

"That's it, Mr. Monk."

"As a matter of interest, what particular commodities did your companies deal in?"

"Do-it-yourself car repair kits; genuine Swedish glass ware; hand-woven Chinese rugs made in Bradford; bargain cameras and binoculars from East Germany; and Japanese pens."

"Quite a range."

"As you say, Mr. Monk, quite a range. And all of them very, very profitable for Mr. Caspar."

"And for you?"

"Less so. I'm not saying I didn't do quite nicely, but considering the profits my share wasn't over-generous. And after all, I was the mug taking the risks. I was the front-line man."

"Why did you stay at it then if you were dissatisfied?"

Butcher let out a long "Ah", stubbed out his cigarette as though trying to bore a hole through the bottom of the ash-tray and said, "In one word, fear. Pure fear." He paused. "Perhaps I'd better explain that, too, but first I could do with another drink."

"Good idea. I'll get them," Richard said, picking up their glasses and moving toward the bar. When he returned Butcher had lit another cigarette and was examining the glowing end as though it were a crystal ball.

"Were you surprised when I said 'fear'?" he asked, looking up.

11

"Not altogether. I've heard that Caspar exercises something of a reign of terror."

"It's probably the finest reign of terror since some of those old kings used to adjust the thumbscrews on their victims themselves." Richard let this somewhat dubious analogy pass with a nod as Butcher went on. "Caspar runs things with a real iron rod. Anyone who kicks over the traces is swiftly dealt with. And by dealt with, I mean physically dealt with. You're lucky if you end up with only a fingernail removed or cigarette burns round your privates or a few teeth knocked down your throat. And because you know you're less lucky if you finish up with a bullet through your guts or being tipped into the river in a weighted sack. Believe me, Mr. Monk, there's nothing the police can do to save you from any of that. They can't stand guard over you round the clock. That's why you keep your mouth shut."

"Which brings us to why you're in Japan and why you think I can help you?" Richard said in the pause which followed.

"Yes," Butcher said in a faraway voice. It was several seconds, however, before he refocused his look on Richard. "I've kicked over the traces in a big way, a really big way. I've flitted with fifty thousand pounds, the total profits of the last business I ran, plus bits kept back from some of the others."

"And you've been carrying this money around with you in cash?"

"Christ no!" Richard was made to feel from his tone as though he had asked Mr. Paul Getty whether he had a money box. "It's in a bank account in Beirut—under an assumed name."

Richard decided not to inquire at this stage how the money had reached a Lebanese bank. Probably it had been smuggled out in cash and humped over the counter in a suitcase at the other end.

"And you did all this without Caspar finding out?" he asked.

"He knows now all right and he must have done his nut when he found out. In fact, I got away only just in time. He'd rumbled something was up a day or two before I left, but I'd gone to ground and they couldn't find me. But both Tendo and Ebony were after me."

"Ebony?"

"Jack Ebony. He's Caspar's other strong-arm boy. Ebony and Tendo do the beatings up."

"How vigorously would Caspar be looking for you?"

"About as vigorously as a hungry shark after a lone swimmer."

"Could he have found out where you are?"

"He not only could have, but he has."

"What makes you say that?"

"Because an attempt was made on my life three nights ago in Tokyo."

Richard gave him a sceptical look. This surely was piling on the dramatics. Caspar might be a major criminal tyrant in his own milieu, but it really was stretching the imagination to be asked to accept that this realm extended to the opposite side of the globe.

"You don't believe me, do you?" Butcher said, reading Richard's expression accurately. "Then let me explain. Caspar has business interests here. Don't ask me what, I don't know. They may even be all above board. They probably are. After all, he has to put his money into something. Anyway, I once met his Japanese agent when he was in London. At least he was introduced as his agent. Seemed a decent little chap, too."

"Have you been in touch with him since you arrived?" Frowning, Butcher shook his head. "Go on telling me about the attempt on your life."

"I first suspected something was up about ten days ago, when I was aware of a little man following me one afternoon. He was so crude, one couldn't fail to notice. Then the same thing happened the next day, but this time it was a different man. It happened two more times, and then last Saturday evening an attempt was made to run me down with a car as I was walking along one of those narrow streets without pavements. This one was a short cut from my hotel to that big main road which runs toward the centre of the city. It was a bloody clumsy attempt and I managed to skip into a doorway, but it was an attempt for all that. I managed to get a glimpse of the two men in the car as it roared past. I've never seen the driver before, but the man beside him was the one whom I'd noticed following me the first time."

"Tokyo traffic is pretty wild . . ." Richard murmured. He still found it difficult to credit that this had been a serious attempt on Butcher's life.

"This was wild driving with a purpose," Butcher replied emphatically. He paused. "And if I'm right—and I know I am —they're certain to have a further try."

Richard found himself automatically glancing round the

bar. The Japanese couple over in the corner had gone and been replaced by a party of four Australians, to judge by their voices. The barman, in his newly starched white jacket and looking as though he'd just been un-gift-wrapped, was busily polishing glasses. If Butcher was in any danger, it didn't appear to be imminent.

"Accepting that you are right," Richard said in a tone full of lawyer's caution, "how on earth can Caspar have traced you to Japan?"

Butcher looked away out of the window. "Through the only person who knew I was coming," he said flatly.

"And who was that?"

"Diane Paisley. She's my girl-friend." In an abstracted voice he added, "I suppose I'd better tell you about her, too. Particularly as she's the main reason for my needing your help." His voice took on a note of bewilderment which had been lacking before. "I met Diane about a year ago and fell in love with her almost at once. Incidentally, she has nothing to do with Caspar and his lot. She works in a boutique in Kensington. Anyway, we were soon courting hard and for the first time in my life I began to think of getting married. Don't run away with the idea that she was the first girl in my life," he said hastily.

Richard smiled. "She just hapened to be the first to stir your chemistry that particular way?"

"Correct."

"Did she know your connection with Caspar?"

"That's how the trouble started. At first she just thought I was in business on my own. Then one evening Tendo turned up at my place when she was there, and afterwards she asked who he was and I told her he worked for the same guy as I did. She just shivered and said he'd given her the creeps, and who was this man I worked for, as she'd understood that I was on my own. Well, I didn't tell her everything straightaway, but bit by bit I gave her most of it. That was after she met Caspar himself."

"How did that come about?"

"He also arrived at my flat one night when she was there. It was obvious that he'd come to look her over. I don't mean to snatch her from me, but just to vet her so to speak. He'd heard I was red hot about her and he wanted to . . . to . . . well, I suppose he wanted to make sure she wouldn't be any sort of a threat. He was all charm to her at the time, but afterwards he made it clear enough to me that both of us could expect nasty trouble if she fell out of line. It was then that I decided deep down that I'd have to break away sooner rather than later. That was about six months ago. Well, it took me the best part of the next four months to work things out. It wasn't easy, believe me, since Caspar keeps an uncomfortably close eye on what's going on. However, I had one or two bits of luck and eventually I was ready to make my flit without a soul having rumbled my intentions." He took a deep breath and expelled it slowly as a long sigh. "A week before the date of my departure, I told Diane of my plan which all along had been made for both of us." He sighed again. "To cut a long story short, we had one helluva row. She said she wouldn't come with me and I told her I'd done it all for her and she must. I did everything I knew to try and persuade her and ... well, even if I wasn't willing to recognise it then, I threw her into a real turmoil, I painted a picture of our starting a new life in another country. I even told her she could make the ruddy choice within limits. I told her I'd buy her a boutique of her own on a palm-fringed island if that was what she'd like; I offered her the lot with myself thrown in. We must have spent almost the whole of that last week talking and arguing, and pleading and shouting and getting nowhere with each other. By the end we were both ready to jump off Waterloo Bridge. God knows how much Scotch and aspirin we didn't consume in that week!"

"Did she know about the fifty thousand pounds?"

"That was the whole bother. She'd have come like a shot if we'd been going to set out like a couple of penniless immigrants." Butcher's tone held a note of grudging respect as well as exasperation. "But I wasn't bloody well prepared to spend the next few years living on bean soup in some foreign garret, and I told her so, I pointed out that I was doing it all for her sake anyway and had run some sizeable risks and I wasn't going to pull the plug on everything just to satisfy a bird's conscience. Even this sucker has his limits, I told her. And that was about the final thing I did say. She walked out on that and I didn't see her again. Two days later I caught a plane." He appeared to sink into morose contemplation of the events he'd been describing. Then in a voice as though he was trying to persuade himself of something he said, "I couldn't do anything else. I'd gone too far. I was committed. Even if I'd wanted to I couldn't have unscrambled the arrangements. It would have been like handing Caspar a revolver and the bullets. And believe me, he wouldn't have said no to the invitation."

A long silence followed during which Richard went over in his mind all that Butcher had told him. "And Diane was the only person who knew where you were going?" he enquired at the end.

"Yes."

"She knew you were coming to Japan?" Butcher nodded. "I don't think you've told me yet, but why did you come to Japan?"

Butcher turned his head and gazed out of the window at the small waterfall which splashed down between clumps of dwarf azaleas into an ornamental pond full of lilies and with three irregularly placed stepping-stones for crossing. Before answering he lit a cigarette with unduly studied motions.

"It was about as far away as I could get from Caspar," he said at length, as though the question were tiresomely irrelevant.

"That all?"

"What do you mean, that all?" he inquired with faint hostility.

"Was distance from England the sole consideration in coming to Japan?"

"I've told you I once met Caspar's man here and I thought I might look him up."

"Because you'd liked what you'd seen of him."

"That's right."

"But you've not been in touch with him?"

"No. I must have got the address wrong. I did try and trace him but without any luck. After that I dropped the idea."

Richard was puzzled. The situation didn't make sense as described by Butcher.

"Weren't you running an unnecessary risk in trying to trace him?" he asked. "After all, isn't he likely to be the very person Caspar has put on your tracks?"

"I suppose he could be," Butcher said in the same uninterested tone. Then, perhaps because he thought he had been rudely unhelpful, he added, "He certainly wasn't one of the men who tailed me, or who was in the car that tried to run me down."

Richard decided to let the matter go at that. Indeed he had no real alternative. He was simply there to listen to whatever Butcher chose to tell him. They hadn't even reached the stage, and possibly never would, of a lawyer-client relationship. They were two English tourists sitting in a Japanese hotel having a pre-dinner drink. To all outward appearances, anyway. It was just that tourists didn't normally approach one another with such life-and-death pleas for help. However, the moment seemed to have arrived for Butcher to lay his final card on the table.

"I'm still not clear," Richard said, "in what way you think I can help you?"

"When are you returning to England, Mr Monk?" Butcher asked quickly.

"In ten days' time."

"May I travel back in the same plane with you?"

Richard shrugged helplessly. "I couldn't stop you doing that even if I wanted to. But what then?"

"Will you be my lawyer when we get home?"

"To what end?"

Butcher moved his empty glass as though it were the queen on a chessboard about to swoop and check-mate his opponent.

"Look, Mr. Monk, anything may happen when I return to England, or at any rate as soon as Caspar learns that I'm back —and that won't be long. I've now told you the whole story and I'd like to feel you're my lawyer and will represent me in any trouble that breaks."

As far as Richard could see the most likely sort of trouble would leave him winding up Butcher's estate. In effect, Butcher was trying to retain him against every eventuality from defending him on some criminal charge to making his funeral arrangements. And God knew what unforeseeable assignments for his lawyer might lie between those two happenings. While he was still wondering exactly how he should reply, Butcher spoke again.

"I told you at the beginning that I was homesick and that's the honest truth. Two months away have made me realise that England's the country I want to live in. I didn't think that a familiar background counted for so much in one's life—in my life, at any rate. But it does and I want to go home, whatever the risks, because I can never be happy anywhere else. Not all on my own." He glanced up at Richard with an expression of implacable determination. "Also I've got to go back and find out what's happened to Diane. I've heard nothing from her since I came away and I'm worried, really worried about her. Caspar knows I'm in Japan and he can only have found it out from her. And she wouldn't have told him that merely for the asking ..." His features became set in a grim mould. "If Caspar or any of his bastards have harmed her, I'll kill him." His tone was coldly practical.

For a few seconds Richard continued to look at him in thoughtful silence. Then, pushing back his chair, he said, "Let's go and have dinner."

3

There was no sign of Butcher in the dining-room the next morning and Richard breakfasted alone. He was grateful for this, since he didn't regard eight o'clock in the morning as other than a time for solitary reflection of the more sombre kind. Despite being physically fit—indeed, some thought he made almost a fetish of physical fitness, furious games of squash, gym work and even an occasional run (after dusk) along Rotten Row—he was not someone who awoke with a cheery smile and an alert mind. And the fact that he was a bachelor and lived alone, and was therefore not obliged to make any effort toward sociable intercourse until after the first terrible hour of each day was over, had left him short of practice in the art of communal breakfasting. He attributed his early morning moroseness to defective metabolism and left it at that.

By the time they had parted company the previous evening, he had agreed in principle to represent Butcher in any forthcoming legal trouble, but had been at pains to emphasise that this was not a binding contract on either of them and that he must reserve the contingent right to decline in the light of a particular event. Butcher had seemed more than satisfied, and Richard realised that it was moral support he was seeking more than anything else at the moment. Except that *moral* was perhaps not quite the right word!

After he had eaten his very conventional breakfast—orange juice, two cups of coffee and a piece of toast spread with apricot jam—he went back to his room, packed his bag and went for a slow stroll in the hotel grounds. There was half an hour to go before they were due to assemble and be borne off on the next stage of their trip.

The cloud had come even lower and long strands gave the impression of having become caught up like dripping veils in the tops of the trees on the opposite slope of the valley.

A large, chauffeur-driven car pulled up at the hotel entrance and Richard watched four Japanese men come out carrying golf clubs. They were middle-aged and on the plump side and wearing dark business suits, which seemed curious attire for golf. But perhaps they changed somewhere before arriving at the first tee. Richard was unaware of the ritual attached to golf in Japan, but knew that the game had become immensely popular and was played with the same fanatical zest that went into building tankers faster than anyone else and generally putting the Japanese hot on the heels of those whom they selected for competition.

He had seen golf practice ranges all over Tokyo. At first he couldn't think what they were, these barren patches of wasteland with their surrounds of high mesh wire, and then one evening he had driven past one when it was floodlit and had seen the line of intent bodies whacking golf balls with the enthusiasm and imprecision of an amateur corps de ballet.

After the golfers had driven away, Richard went over and sat on a low parapet from which he could look down on an ornamental garden such as abound in Japan, and which yet never fail to give a cherished appearance. While he was there, the Indian couple came out of the hotel and strolled across. Richard rose.

"Good morning, Mr. Monk. You slept well, I trust."

"Excellently. And you, too, I hope." He looked from one to the other while expressing this pious sentiment.

"Thank you, yes," Mr. Lal said. Mrs. Lal merely smiled enigmatically. "It is quite like parts of Kashmir this district here," Mr. Lal went on with a wave of his hand which took in the whole three hundred and sixty degrees.

Richard laughed. "I'd been thinking how it resembled bits of Switzerland."

Mr. Lal smiled broadly. "All we do when we travel is liken what we see to some other part of the world. It is the human need always to make comparisons and so to anchor experience. Why can't we just say, it is beautiful, it is unique, it is Japan?"

Before Richard could get caught up in these interesting philosophical eddies, the two French Canadians passed by and further matutinal greetings were exchanged. Shortly after this, Butcher himself appeared and the group was complete.

"Morning all," he said cheerfully, giving Richard a conspiratorial wink. "I call this pretty good us all being ready before the bus arrives."

"Perhaps we are beginning to succumb to the Japanese influence of orderliness," Mr. Lal said. "It is all a question of mental approach and of becoming attuned to the ways of our hosts."

Mrs. Lal turned on another of her enigmatic smiles, but otherwise no one seemed disposed to react to this challenging proposition.

At nearly five minutes before the scheduled time of departure two cars swung through the gate and halted before the entrance. A young man jumped out of the first and came over to them.

"Good morning, ladies and gentlemen, I have come to guide you to the train." He beamed around him. "I am so happy you are with us today and I hope you will have many pleasant times with Japan Travel Bureau. And now, if you will place yourselves in the cars we will position your luggage and go to the station where you will take the New Tokaido Limited Express to Kyoto."

Twenty-five minutes later, he had them drawn up on the platform of Odawara station waiting for the train.

"The New Tokaido Line was opened in time for the Olympic Games. It is an all new railway line which goes from Tokyo to Osaka. The super express trains take three hours and ten minutes to travel the five hundred and fifteen kilometres. The super express trains stop only at Nagoya and Kyoto. You take the limited express train which stops other places." Proudly he added, "But you come back to Tokyo by the super express train."

At that moment one of these hurtled through on the centre track and almost sucked them off the platform in its slipstream.

"Goes like a bloody missile," Butcher observed.

A little later, after their guide had supplied them with a few more details on the New Tokaido Line and had apologized for the continuing non-appearance of Mount Fuji, their train (it did indeed resemble a blue and cream missile on wheels) glided to a halt at the platform. Apparently miraculously, they found themselves directly opposite the door to the coach in which their seats were reserved.

"Good-bye, good-bye," caroled their guide, as he hopped back on to the platform just before the train pulled out. "Happy journeys. Have no fears, a new guide will greet you at Kyoto."

With astonishing acceleration and without any noise, the train was in no time cleaving its way across the landscape.

Butcher had insisted that Richard should take the window

seat since he said it would be wasted on him as trains always sent him to sleep.

"Anyway," he had added, "in one sense, I'm only coming along for the ride."

The journey passed quickly. From time to time lengthy announcements in Japanese came over the loudspeaker system, followed on occasions by what appeared to be a severely truncated version in English. Several times they were thanked for travelling on the New Tokaido Line and once for not using the lavatory. Throughout the trip a team of smiling girls passed up and down the train selling fruit and sandwiches as well as coffee and soft drinks and ice cream.

Long before they reached Kyoto, the sky had cleared and a brassy-looking sun shone out of a canopy of pure blue.

Butcher slept until the last half hour when he woke up, had a prodigious stretch and was suddenly one hundred per cent alive.

"Looks like it's quite warm outside," he said.

Richard nodded. "We've been travelling south all the time, so there should be a difference."

"What is this place Kyoto?"

"It's the ancient capital of Japan."

"Strikes me they say that of every other town you visit."

Richard laughed. "I agree, they do seem to have had a fair number of capitals."

"How far is it from Osaka?"

"Only about thirty miles, I think. If as much."

"Good! An American I met in Tokyo was telling me there are some pretty interesting night spots there. We might go in one evening."

"Hmm," Richard murmured non-commitally.

The train slid into another of the cavernous new stations which had been built along the New Tokaido Line and came to a halt. As it did so, Richard saw one of the Travel Bureau's ubiquitous young men waiting in exactly the right place.

"Hello, hello there," he greeted them as they stepped out on the platform. "Please to come with me and we go to hotel. My colleague attends to luggage." He indicated another beaming young man who was already handing their cases to a porter.

They had just begun to follow him along the platform when Butcher clutched at Richard's sleeve and said, "Look, that man just about to go down the steps. The one on the left."

All Richard saw when he had focused his gaze in the right

direction was the back of a head disappearing down the exit staircase. He turned back to Butcher to find that all the colour had drained from his face.

"I swear he was one of the men who followed me in Tokyo. He must have got off the train, too. He was standing at the top of the staircase looking straight at us until I spotted him."

Richard pursed his lips. The trouble was he'd not seen sufficient to draw any conclusions.

"I would think the odds are you're mistaken," he said, cautiously.

Butcher shook his head. "It was the same man all right."

Richard said nothing more. If, indeed, Butcher was being watched, it was obvious that they'd have had no difficulty in trailing him to Kyoto. The question was whether they would make another attempt on his life while he was here. Richard fervently hoped not and was honest enough to admit to himself that he was not thinking solely of Butcher.

It was with a distinct feeling of unease that he gazed out on the crowds thronging the arcaded pavements of Kyoto's main street. It suddenly required no effort to see a potential assassin behind every face.

When they arrived at the hotel, Butcher suggested that he and Richard should lunch together in the coffee shop. It was almost empty and its utterly un-Japanese atmosphere seemed to have a relaxing effect on Butcher. A hamburger, followed by ice-cream, further assisted the process, though he looked askance at Richard's plate of sushi and cup of green tea.

"Isn't that that raw fish muck?" he inquired as Richard popped a morsel into his mouth.

"Not all of it. This is seaweed and that's a piece of ginger."

"I don't know how you can eat it."

"Haven't you tried any Japanese food since you've been here?"

"Not if I can help it. Had that sukiyaki once. I suppose it wasn't too bad, except the bits of meat kept falling off my chopsticks. I was ruddy hungry afterwards. Went straight back to the hotel and had egg and chips up in my room. And as for that green tea you're drinking," he went on, "it's just like ditch-water."

"Very fragrant ditch-water," Richard remarked.

"What are you going to do this afternoon, Mr. Monk?" Butcher asked, their meal finished.

"I was proposing to stroll about the town."

Richard led the way to a small restaurant in the Gion district which he had noticed on his afternoon walk.

"Place looks good at night," Butcher remarked, gazing around at the coruscating neon, which managed to give every Japanese city a new life after dark.

They dived down a narrow alley hung with lanterns and brightly lit signs and of tumultuous cooking smells.

"This is it," Richard said, turning into one of the numerous doorways.

Butcher took a quick look about him before following Richard inside, where they removed their shoes and put on slippers supplied by the house.

"Don't fancy myself in these if we have to make a quick getaway," Butcher muttered.

"Forget all that and enjoy your dinner. I'll be your food-taster if you want one." Nevertheless, Richard was relieved when Butcher became patently distracted from his more sombre thoughts by the presence of the very pretty girl who served them. This involved not only putting the food on their plates but cooking it on the conical grill which rose up like a volcano in the centre of their table. As items of food became cooked she would drop them in the small bowls of soya sauce which each had in front of him.

"Just like a mother bird feeding her chicks," Butcher remarked as she smilingly dropped a bamboo shoot into his bowl.

At the start they had tried to make conversation with her, but her English consisted of no more than the first line of two English pop numbers and this was limiting. After she had repeated, "It's been a hard day's night" and "We all live in a yellow submarine" each three times, the smiles on their faces had tended to solidify and communication had lapsed apart from nods and smiles and an attempted pat on her behind from Butcher, which she had nimbly avoided.

Toward the end of the meal, when she had temporarily retired from the table, Butcher said, "I don't want Caspar to find out that I've returned to England, so we may have to act a bit cunning before we leave Japan. You won't mind, will you?"

"What do you have in mind?"

"Changing our flight at the last moment. Something of that sort. The real point is to prevent Caspar being sent details of our journey home."

24

"Our?"

"He'll soon know that I've met you."

"You make him sound even more powerful than I'd supposed."

"He's got a good organisation," Butcher observed flatly.

"Does he have a wife?" Richard inquired.

Butcher nodded. "Paula. She's quite a doll."

"What part does she play in his affairs?"

"Not much more than live off the proceeds."

"Any children?"

"No. If there had been, they'd have been born with steel chips in their bloodstream. Paula Caspar was moulded in an iron foundry."

"How does she get on with her husband?"

"Rumour is that it's live and let live."

"Does he have other women then?"

"I couldn't tell you, Mr. Monk. He's as discreet as a cat about some things and that's one of them."

"What does the household consist of? Just Caspar and his wife?"

"A sister of hers acts as a sort of housekeeper at the place near Weybridge, and either Ebony or Tendo acts at chauffeur when required. Mrs. Caspar spends most of the time down at Weybridge but he often stops at their flat near Baker Street."

When the girl returned, it was to bring them their bill and to indicate that she was ready to go off duty. Butcher gave her a long predatory look as she waited for them to settle up and hopefully tried to find out where she lived. All he achieved, however, was the address of the restaurant which she laboriously wrote down for him. He tore the piece of paper up with a snort as soon as she had departed.

"Must be a country girl," he said disgustedly. "The city birds are far less coy." He ran his tongue vigorously round his teeth. "I seem to have got half the meal caught up round my gums." Then lighting a cigarette he said, "What are we going to do now?"

"What do you want to do?" Richard asked, mentally keeping the options open.

"I wouldn't mind taking a look around the town. Perhaps we could find a night spot where the girls know what girls ought to know. If it's anything like Tokyo, there's fun to be had round some corner or other." He paused and gave Richard a quizzical glance. "By the way, you're not married, are you?"

"No."

"That's all right then. Not that I'm suggesting it wouldn't have been otherwise. After all, if you happen to be one side of the world when your wife's the other . . ."

Richard was on the verge of replying, but refrained. He didn't feel in the mood to argue sexual morality with someone whose morals were obviously different from his own. Not that he thought of himself as a puritan in such matters. Indeed, he wasn't one, it was more a question of natural discretion. Furthermore, all his lawyer's caution warned him against becoming involved in any situation which Butcher might subsequently be tempted to exploit to his own advantage. The artificiality of their present relationship also held its own dangers for the future. He wasn't going to have Butcher knocking on his private front door at all hours as a result of a night out together in Kyoto. Richard had never cared for mixing business with pleasure, and made a point of trying to keep his professional and his social life apart.

They had left the restaurant and were walking back toward the main road when Butcher suddenly asked, "Ever played Pachinko?"

"Several times."

"Let's go and find a place."

"That shouldn't be hard." Pachinko, a pinball game, could almost be described as a national drug. Somewhere Richard had seen staggering statistics showing the extent to which the Japanese people had fallen under its hypnotic influence. Moreover, it was not difficult to accept these when you walked down any street in the entertainment quarter of any town. Pachinko saloons abounded like stalls in a market place and were always packed with players in various degrees of hypnosis.

There was nothing to choose between them and they entered the first saloon they came across, with its serried rows of vertical pachinko machines. Although music was blaring out from several loudspeakers, it was all but submerged under the din of steel balls flying round the frames of the boards and dropping into cups or falling back out of play.

"Just like being in a noisy factory," Richard said, as he and Butcher walked down one of the aisles looking for two free machines.

"Think of the profits someone's making," Butcher replied in a tone which caused Richard to glance at him sharply. But he had stationed himself in front of a machine and already begun feeding in the supply of metal balls he had purchased. On the far side of him was a youth who gave every appearance of being an automaton. His expression was fixed and his operating hand worked with the speed of a precision jig. Richard reckoned he fed the metal balls into the machine at the rate of one a second. Feeling, by comparison, like a clumsy yokel on a ballroom floor he began to play himself.

Twenty minutes later, several hundred yen poorer and with hands black from handling the metal balls, they made their way out, pausing only to wash at the basins provided for that purpose by a thoughtful management.

"Only the Japanese would think of having public washing facilities in an amusement arcade," Richard said.

"Have you been to their public baths?" Butcher inquired. Richard shook his head. "Trouble is they've closed down most of the mixed ones," he added sadly.

They emerged on to the pavement and looked across at an equally jam-packed pachinko saloon on the opposite side of the road.

"I imagine some Japanese Caspar has probably muscled in on the pachinko concession," Richard remarked. Butcher grinned.

They strolled down toward a busy crossroads and waited on the edge of the pavement for the lights to change. Richard was gazing at an extremely attractive girl sitting in a first-floor window opposite when he heard Butcher let out a shout and at the same moment was aware of a car horn being frantically sounded. In the same split second he saw the car swerve wildly out toward the middle of the road and Butcher pick himself up and step back on to the pavement.

"I was pushed," he gasped out. "Some murdering bastard tried to push me in front of that car."

Richard looked rapidly about him. There were now a dozen or more people waiting to cross. They gazed at Butcher with mild curiosity, and one or two of them giggled as he brushed himself down.

"Anyone see what happened?" Richard asked, helplessly.

Either they were all part of the conspiracy or, more likely, no one had. A second later the lights changed and the crowd flowed on, leaving Richard and Butcher standing alone.

"Let's go back to the hotel," Butcher said in a shaken voice. On the way he asked, "You didn't see who it was?"

"I'm afraid not. Whoever it was must have got away under cover of the crowd."

"Well, if they're reckoning on third time lucky, they can reckon again. I'm taking bloody good care there won't be a third time."

This was hardly the moment to mention it, but Richard couldn't help reflecting that, assuming these had been deliberate attempts on Butcher's life, they were singularly inept.

On the other hand he was forced to conclude that someone had had them under observation the whole evening, awaiting the opportunity to kill Butcher in a seemingly accidental way. It was a disturbing thought.

4

"Nara, national capital of Japan during the eighth century," Richard read in the leaflet he had collected at some stage of his trip. He was sitting in the bus outside the hotel waiting to go there for the day. To his relief Butcher had decided to remain in Kyoto and not accompany him on the outing. He had never heard of Nara, wanted no part of it and was determined to stray no further from his bedroom than necessity or boredom dictated. He had given Richard a long-suffering look on being told of yet another capital of ancient Japan.

It was a glorious day and Richard thoroughly enjoyed the hour's drive. On the bus he found himself sitting next to a pleasant young Australian with whom he swapped impressions.

The guide on this occasion was a woman. She had a bland, moonlike face with a large mouth and protruding eyes which were afflicted by a constant nervous blink. She spoke grammatical English which was perfectly intelligible for eighty per cent of the time so that Richard was doubly bothered by the regular dive into unintelligibility for the other twenty per cent. He also found her evoking a strange, and probably quite superfluous compassion in him. She had a tired, beaten, but unbeatable, look which made him want to help her in some way.

He mentioned this to his companion who gave her a quick glance and said crisply, "She reminds me of the sadistic old cow who taught at my kindergarten. She had poppy eyes and a mouth like a mine-shaft."

Richard grinned. "Well, I'd sooner think our guide was a sadistic old cow than that she's tired and sad."

They arrived at Nara and embarked upon the usual tour of shrines, the first of which was situated in a park full of sacred and extremely tame deer. These followed visitors about giving them violent nudges to indicate that sacredness did nothing for the appetite. Richard fed them the rather pleasant-smelling biscuits which could be bought for the purpose. As he did so he found himself wondering whether there were not possibilities for Caspar in a "deer biscuit" racket. So much for a couple of days in Butcher's company, he'd begun to see everything within a context of criminal enterprise. What was more, he now realised that the unheralded entry into his life of the fugitive from Caspar's justice had subtly but effectively queered the remainder of his holiday. Even in this short space of time he had been forced to assume a degree of responsibility for Butcher. And last night's incident had done nothing to lessen it.

It was around five o'clock when they arrived back in Kyoto and Richard felt a sudden tension as he walked through the swing doors of the hotel. Just supposing something had happened to Butcher while he had been out . . .

But the lobby looked reassuringly normal. The clerk at the reception desk gave him a respectful nod as he handed him the key.

"Is Mr. Butcher up in his room?" Richard asked, despite himself.

The clerk turned to the honeycomb of slots behind him. "Mr. Butcher is out, sir," he said gravely.

"You don't happen to remember what time he went out?" Richard asked, cursing himself for the upsurge of nervousness.

"No, sir," the clerk replied.

He was about to get into the lift when he heard his name called.

"Hello there, Mr. Monk, you back already?"

Butcher was sitting over in a far corner of the lobby with a glass of beer in front of him. Richard went across and flopped down beside him.

"Join me in a beer?"

"I certainly will."

"You look quite exhausted."

"Shrines and temples are pretty tough on the feet," Richard replied. "What sort of a day have you had?"

"I've been sitting here most of the time just watching people."

"Nothing further's happened?"

Butcher shook his head. "I reckon I'm safe indoors. They seem to be hit and run types. I guess they're scared of meeting me face to face." Butcher patted the bulge made by his gun.

Richard thought this was a reasonable inference on the evidence. He certainly hoped it to be so.

30

"You're not going out again today, are you?" Butcher inquired with a sudden change of mood.

"There's a geisha party slated for this evening."

"And you're going?"

"What about you?"

"Have you seen any geisha girls?" Butcher's tone was indignant. "They look just like circus clowns and could be anything from nineteen to ninety.

Richard surmised that Butcher's disillusionment was more probably due to the discovery that geisha girls were highly trained and respectable exponents of an ancient art and not, as he might have previously thought, birds to be got between the sheets for a bit of friendly massage.

It was remarkable that Butcher could ever have imagined himself settling down in Japan or in any other foreign country for that matter. He was as British as sausages and mash and about as unexportable.

The sooner he returned to England, the better. Whatever the danger that awaited him there.

The next day they travelled back to Tokyo in one of the lauded super-expresses. As they stood on the platform of Kyoto Station waiting for it to come in, Butcher kept glancing uneasily about him. He also, Richard noticed, kept a safe distance back from the edge of the platform, which was perhaps a sensible precaution when one thought about it. Only two days before, Richard had read a newspaper item on the number of people who had been killed by the trains of the New Tokaido Line. Admittedly, none of them appeared to have been cases of murder, nor, for that matter, had they been accidental deaths. The grim fact was that jumping in front of the expresses had become a fashionable form of suicide. The article which Richard had read had been sparked off by the self-immolating leap of a seventeen-year-old boy on learning that he had failed his exams.

The train slithered silently into the station and one of the Travel Bureau's helpful young men found them their seats, and as quickly bowed himself out of their lives. They were now on their own, the Indian couple and the two French-Canadians having left that morning to visit Hiroshima.

During the three-hour journey, Butcher sat back in his seat with eyes closed while Richard gazed out on the ever-changing landscape which whipped past the window as though someone was running away with it in the other direction.

Butcher came to as they were snaking through the outer fringes of Tokyo.

"You don't mind if I book in at your hotel, do you?" he asked.

Richard, who had been half-expecting him to make the suggestion, shook his head.

An announcement in English informed them that they would be arriving at Tokyo Central Station in three minutes' time and he thanked them for taking the train.

Butcher insisted that Richard get out first and then kept very close to his side at they plunged into the bustling labyrinth of one of the busiest stations in the world.

They found a cab easily, though Butcher refused to take the first one which drove up, to the baffled annoyance of the driver.

Richard felt a bit like a nursemaid hurrying home with a charge who was rapidly sickening for measles. His own relief measured Butcher's when eventually they were in an apparently innocent taxi and on their way to the hotel.

It was a further relief to Richard when the hotel was able to provide Butcher with a room, if only because propinquity solved more difficulties than it created.

"When do we fly home, Mr. Monk?" Butcher asked, as they followed a bell-boy down a corridor.

"I'm ready to leave the day after tomorrow if you wish," Richard replied.

Butcher pursed his lips thoughtfully. "Mind if I come in for a moment?" he asked as they arrived at the door of Richard's room. Inside he pulled an airline timetable out of his pocket and began studying it. "Incidentally, which way is your ticket routed?" he asked after a frowning silence.

"Over the pole."

"Good. Couldn't be better! I was hoping it was." His head moved as if he were reading a piece of music to time.

"There's a J.A.L. flight direct to London the day after tomorrow so let's get reservations on that." He threw the time-table down. "If you don't mind making the arrangements for both of us over the telephone with the airline office, I shall go to the hotel travel bureau and ask them to book me on an Air France flight to Paris, leaving two days later. Is that O.K.?"

"I suppose so," Richard replied dubiously.

"Well, I'm not asking you to do anything illegal, am I?"

Butcher said a trifle testily. "I'll give you the money for my ticket. You won't have to pay my fare home if that's what's worrying you."

"It's just that I don't care for all this deviousness."

Butcher looked at him in amazement, then grinned. "And you a lawyer, Mr. Monk!"

"There's deviousness and deviousness," Richard said.

"The only purpose of this so-called deviousness is to give me a better chance of arriving back in one piece; and of staying that way after I have arrived."

There was silence for a second or two before Richard said, "That's settled then. We fly by J.A.L. the day after tomorrow."

The next morning Richard completed his side of things without meeting any problems. He decided that, from now on, the fewer questions he asked, the better, though he felt it necessary to warn Butcher not to do anything by way of covering his tracks which could embroil his lawyer.

"Don't worry, Mr. Monk," he had replied. "As far as I'm concerned you're more precious than a life-buoy to a shipwrecked sailor. I've got more sense than to queer your pitch. If I fall into trouble, I want you to get me out of it, not be in there with me."

During those last two days, Butcher hardly stirred out of the hotel, though he made a point of being seen about in the public parts of it. Richard spent most of his time in last-minute shopping and in re-visiting those bits of the city which had particularly pleased him. The sad truth was, however, that Tokyo was no longer the same place it had been six days before. Butcher's emergence into his life had seen to that. It was as though he now dragged a ball and chain with him wherever he went. Even the silent ramparts of the Imperial Palace seemed to take on a different perspective. Not for the first time he silently cursed Butcher for his unwanted intervention; yet even as he did so he felt the almost sensual tingle which he invariably experienced on the threshold of a big case.

The best pilots are said to fly via the seat of their pants; Richard, for his part, knew whether a case was going to develop by a preliminary tingle in his bloodstream. It wasn't infallible, but it was a useful barometer.

When he got back to the hotel about six o'clock on the evening before departure, the desk clerk handed him a letter with his room key. His first thought was that it must be in connection with their flight arrangements, but a second's reflection told him that this was not a business envelope, moreover it was hand-addressed and not typewritten. It bore no stamp and so had presumably also been delivered by hand.

Puzzled and curious, he slit the envelope open and pulled out a piece of singly folded matching paper and read:

"Dear Mr. Monk,
I read you are famous English lawyer visiting Tokyo.
Please will you see me.
I will be in the Tanacho Bar near Shinjuku Station at 8 clocks all evenings until hope fades.

Obediently,
A. Shima."

He returned to the desk. "Do you happen to know when this letter arrived?"

The clerk took the envelope from Richard and went and spoke to somebody out of sight.

"I think it was while you were away in Kyoto, Mr. Monk. Unfortunately, it was placed in the box of your old room number and so you did not receive it when you returned last night. For this please accept our many apologies. It was a most regrettable error."

"Don't worry about that, I'm not complaining, I only wanted to know when it arrived since it has no date on it."

"That, too, is regrettable," the desk clerk remarked gravely.

Richard re-read the letter as he went up in the lift. It was clear what had happened. A few days after his arrival in Tokyo a Japanese journalist who was the friend of an English friend had called at the hotel and they had had a drink together, followed by dinner a couple of nights later. The journalist had asked if Richard had any objection to mention being made of his visit in the gossip column of an English language newspaper with which he was connected, and Richard had said that he hadn't and had thought no more about it. This must have been the item which A. Shima had seen. But when? And how many evenings had he—or could it be she?—spent waiting at the Tanacho Bar? Had hope faded?

There was something pathetic, but direct, in the plea. Something which would have turned denial into harsh rejection. This was his last night in Tokyo and he had no particular ideas for spending it, so why not a visit to the Tanacho Bar? By the time he had reached his room, he had made up his mind. He had also decided that he was not going to let Butcher in on his plans.

It was five minutes to eight when he emerged from Shinjuku subway station into the maelstrom of Tokyo's most popular entertainment district for the Japanese themselves. Music blared out of numerous cafés whose interiors were as ill-lit as their exteriors dazzled the eye with flashing neon, and hot, spicy cooking smells filled the air.

Richard knew from previous experience of Tokyo that it was one thing to arrive in the area of your destination, and quite another to identify the actual place you wanted. One might say that one eventually arrived despite, rather than by virtue of, the multitude of directions sought and helpfully given. On this occasion, it took him a quarter of an hour to track down the Tanacho Bar which he subsequently estimated to be approximately two hundred yards from his starting point.

After a moment of sudden apprehension when he eventually found himself on the pavement outside, he passed through the door and gazed about him trying to accustom his eyes to the shadowy gloom within.

A hostess in a golden lamé dress led him smiling to a table against the wall in the depths of the interior. She took his order for a beer and moved away. Richard noticed three other similarly dressed girls standing together in one corner. They eyed him with polite interest. There weren't a great number of customers present and certainly no one alone who might be A. Shima. It seemed probable that hope must have faded after all.

While he was still peering about him, his beer arrived. He became aware that the girl who had brought it was still hovering by the table and he turned his head to look at her. She was younger than the others and had an air of sweet innocence which, by contrast, made the gold lamé outfit look meretricious on her.

"Mr. Monk?" she asked in a nervous whisper.

"Yes." He stared at her disbelievingly. "Are you ; . . Miss Shima?"

She nodded. "It is nice that you come. I may talk to you, yes?" As if she read his thoughts she went on, "It is all right, it is allowed. We entertain and then you will buy another drink. It is the business."

"In that case, let me buy you a drink and then we can drink and talk together."

"No. I just talk, not drink." She sat down at the table. "You *are* famous lawyer, Mr. Monk?"

"Just say I'm a lawyer!"

She pulled from a small bag, made of the same material as her dress, a newspaper cutting and pushed it across the table. He read it and passed it back. It was the usual sort of puff that appears in such columns. He noticed that it also mentioned where he was staying.

"It is you?" she inquired.

"Yes, but exaggerated."

She looked uncomprehending. "I may talk to you?" she repeated.

"Please do."

"It is about my brother. He has disappeared. I think he is now dead."

Richard tried to look sympathetic, at the same time wondering what this had to do with him.

"My brother went to England last year."

"You mean he disappeared in England?"

"No, he came back to Japan and then he disappear." Richard nodded and waited. Whatever he was expecting, it was not what followed. "You know Mr. Caspar in England?"

He felt a jolt as though a gun had been jabbed into his ribs. When he had recovered from his initial shock, he said in a tone as neutral as he could make it, "I have heard of him, but I don't know him personally."

"He is a wicked man." Richard wasn't sure whether this was meant as a statement or a question, so maintained silence. "My brother work in Japan for this Mr. Caspar. Then he disappear and now another Japanese man work for Mr. Caspar. This other man visit my brother and soon after that he disappear and I hear already that he is dead."

"What is the name of this other man?" Richard asked.

"I not know. But he is wicked man, too. He tell me to ask no questions about my brother or he will hurt me."

"So you have met him?"

"No. On telephone he tell me this."

"And how do you believe I can help you?" Richard inquired, peculiarly conscious of the familiarity of his question.

"Perhaps you can find out from this Mr. Caspar what he knows about my brother. My father is old and he worries about him. He does not know that he was mixed up with bad men. I know, but my father does not know. He believes my brother is in England now. I tell him that he is there perhaps. But, Mr. Monk, we must know what has happened to my brother and you can find out, yes?"

"If I do find anything out, I will write to you," Richard replied quietly. "What is your address?"

He handed her his diary and indicated a page on which she should note it down.

Soon afterwards, she rose, gave him a formal bow and disappeared through a service door. He left before she came back again.

He walked in a daze along the crowded pavement pondering the incredible coincidence sprung by his visit to the Tanacho Bar. And it couldn't be anything other than coincidence. Miss Shima had simply seen his presence in Tokyo as an opportunity of pulling aside some of the dark veils which surrounded her brother's mysterious disappearance. He had been no more than a fortuitous answer to an earnest prayer.

What seemed a fair deduction was that Caspar's Japanese agent, whom Butcher had described as "a decent little chap", was Miss Shima's brother. The man whom Butcher had halfheartedly tried to trace but whose address he had said he must have got wrong.

Richard found that he was still trying to make sense out of it when he arrived back at the hotel. Butcher who was sitting in the lobby jumped up and came over.

"This time tomorrow we'll be airborne."

"With luck," Richard added automatically.

While they were having a drink, Richard said. "You mentioned Caspar's agent in Tokyo a few days ago. What did you tell me his name was?"

"I don't think I did," Butcher said warily. "That was the trouble, I had a wrong address and I'd forgotten his name and so I couldn't get in touch with him. Why?"

"I'd been wondering whether there was any chance of finding out a bit more about the people who've made these attempts on your life."

"By this time tomorrow night, we can forget about them," Butcher said. "Incidentally, we'll have to make our way to the airport separately and you probably won't see me until you're actually on the plane ..."

And so it proved to be. Indeed, Richard had begun to fear that Butcher was going to miss the plane when he suddenly appeared at the top of the gangway. He looked as if he had been running hard, and he flopped into the seat behind Richard and immediately ordered a large Scotch, followed by another as Haneda Airport dropped behind them.

The sixteen-hour flight passed in a sort of euphoric nightmare. Food and drink came in great quantities and at regular intervals and the sun shone down on an endless snowy wasteland. Then just when it seemed that the cycles of food and drink, coupled with restless dozing, would go on for ever, they made their descent to Heathrow Airport. They had just finished dinner and in London it was breakfast time.

By pre-arrangement he and Butcher made no contact with one another after landing.

"I'll be getting in touch with you shortly, Mr. Monk," Butcher had said gravely as they taxied up to the terminal.

Despite a feeling of utter disorientation after a journey which had made mockery of time, Richard had still experienced a curious physical tingle as part of his mind addressed itself to what might lie ahead.

5

It was shortly after nine o'clock when Richard let himself into his flat and gave a silent sigh of satisfaction at being home again. In a few weeks time his wanderlust would be stirring once more, but for the moment it was lovely to be back.

He was still standing in the passage when Mrs. Fleet, his faithful daily help, came out of his bedroom. She was loyal, unimaginative and entirely practical, so that even though he had been on the other side of the world for a month, she wasted no time on the customary pleasantries of reunion.

"I've just been putting two hot-water bottles in your bed to air it. I expect you'd like some breakfast?"

"No thanks, Mrs. Fleet. I couldn't eat anything at the moment."

"Will you be staying home for lunch?"

Richard winced inwardly. "I don't think I'll even want anything to eat then."

Mrs. Fleet gave him an appraising look. "It's probably all that foreign cooking that's upset you."

"I'm not upset in that sense. Just travel-weary after sixteen hours in an aeroplane."

There was no point in trying to explain to Mrs. Fleet about the changes in time involved in such a journey as he had just made. He had on one occasion attempted to make her understand that New York time was five hours behind London's. He had done this at ten o'clock on a winter's morning and her only reaction had been to comment that she wouldn't like such long, dark nights.

"I've got the kettle on. Shall I make a cup of tea?"

"That's a splendid idea," Richard murmured, picking up his cases and going into his bedroom. A few minutes later he entered the kitchen and handed over the present he had brought her from Japan.

It was an attractive fan and she examined it impassively. Then obviously feeling that some comment was required of her, she said, "You don't often see fans these days."

39

"You do in Japan," Richard said in a jollying tone.

"I expect they have the sort of weather for them. But it's quite pretty, isn't it?"

"I'm glad you like it," he observed, and left the kitchen before she could tell him, as he was sure she would, that it would make a nice plaything for one of her grandchildren. It was always uppermost in his mind when he gave her a present that it was the thought which really counted.

He looked round the sitting-room with a fond eye. Despite what friends had told him, he hadn't yet tired of his ultra-modern Scandinavian furniture. As for the black leather chair which resembled a sawn-off egg, it was heavenly to sit in, and looked undeniably striking on its base of furry white rug. He now flung himself into its capacious depth and awaited the tea. After that, he would glance through his mail, phone the office to annouce his return, not that he had any intention of going in till tomorrow, and then probably stretch out on his bed for a couple of hours.

"Those are lovely roses," he said when she entered with the tray. "Where'd you get them, in the market?"

She looked at him in surprise. "I wouldn't waste your money buying roses," she said trenchantly, "Miss Wyatt brought those round yesterday. They were all wrapped up in that cellophane paper, but I thought I had better put them in water after she'd gone."

"They're certainly very pretty."

"Yes, they're quite nice," she conceded.

After she had gone out of the room, Richard gazed at the roses and turned his mind to the donor. He was still uncertain quite how he felt about Sarah Wyatt. He had first met her three months ago and they'd been out a few times together and got on well. On the other hand he had regarded his trip to Japan as coming at just the right moment to enable him to take stock of their relationship and decide whether or not he wished it to develop, And to give him his due, he *had* thought about her quite a bit before Butcher's intrusion drove most other things out of his mind. He had sent her a couple of postcards and brought her a fan, too. A rather more orna-mental and expensive one than he had given Mrs. Fleet.

But what should one think of a girl-friend who greeted your arrival home with roses! Even if she did work in something called a flower boutique!

He was still pondering the implications when he dropped

off to sleep. It was early afternoon when he awoke and, after a bath, he felt ready to grasp what was left of the day. His first move was to phone the Scarbys. Jane answered.

"Hello, Richard, when did you get back?" She sounded thrilled to hear his voice.

"This morning. How are all the Scarbys?"

"I shan't tell you. You can come and find out for yourself."

"I was hoping you'd say that. May I look in this evening?"

"Come to supper. Alan said he'd be back around seven. He's at Hertford Assizes today. Why don't you come along early, Richard? You can entertain me and Sophie until I put her to bed."

"I'll bring my samisen to the party."

"Is that one of those twangy Japanese instruments?"

"Yes."

"I thought it was. In that event, you'll learn the hard way like the lady who took her harp to a party."

Jane Scarby had been a moderately successful model before marrying Alan three years ago. Now she was an utterly happy wife and mother, living in a Victorian terrace house in Fulham. Though well removed from the bread line, the Scarbys had only Alan's earnings at the Bar to live on and it was a measure of the strength of his and Richard's friendship that it had completely survived Richard's sudden acquisition of great wealth, together with the inevitable changes this had brought in his life.

After speaking to Jane Scarby, Richard telephoned his office and spoke to Roy Harding, who had been out when he called in the course of the morning. Roy was his salaried partner and looked after most of the civil work, leaving Richard to indulge his interest in matters criminal. It was an ideal working arrangement which Richard never ceased to acknowledge. Harding was four years older than himself and, at the same time his employee, but thanks to a complete compatability of temperaments the obvious points of friction just never arose.

For fifteen minutes they exchanged news, though for most of this time Harding was giving him a run-down on the firm's activities during his absence.

"Sheila will be pleased to see you back, Richard," he said at the end. Sheila Gillam was Richard's secretary.

"I'm glad to hear it, but why?"

"I've been using her to help me out and she finds wills and conveyances dreary fodder compared with the protein diet you provide."

Richard laughed. "You haven't forgotten what happened when I borrowed that late secretary of yours, Gloria Something-or-other? She came out in a nervous rash and blamed me."

"Well, it was the details of a particularly filthy rape case you were dictating."

"But who'd have thought that would upset Gloria by the look of her? I've always suspected that the intimacies of a good trust deed would have had the same effect on her that day. Come hell or high water she was going to break into a rash and she decided to fasten it on to me ... Anyway, Roy, see you tomorrow."

"Fine, Richard. We'll have the 'Welcome Back, Boss' banner unfurled."

About half past four Richard went to the garage where he kept his Mercedes 250 SL. Mrs. Fleet's son, who was a motor mechanic, looked after it in his spare time and had spent the previous Sunday afternoon getting it ready for Richard's return. This had included giving it a wax shampoo, so that it now had a show-room gloss.

Jane Scarby was giving her daughter tea when Richard arrived. She embraced him warmly and he, in turn, kissed the top of his god-daughter's head, stepping back smartly to avoid her jammy fingers as they tried to clutch his sleeve.

"Sit down out of Sophie's reach and tell me about Japan," Jane said, settling herself back beside her daughter. "For a start, is Mount Fuji as mystical as it always looks in pictures?"

"I'll have to go back another time to be able to answer that," Richard replied, and went on to explain his frustration and failure to get a proper view of the sacred mountain.

"Rather like going to Rome and not seeing St. Peter's," she said. "Well, tell me about Japanese women, and don't say the whole land was blanketed in fog the whole time you were there and that you only heard their footsteps."

For the next twenty minutes they conversed animatedly. Then when Sophie had finished eating and been sponged clean she was let loose on Richard while Jane cleared the table. It was at this psychological moment that he produced the present he had brought her, a stuffed creature with an engaging leer, known as Oba-Q-Chan. He also handed to Jane the kimono he had purchased on his last day in Tokyo.

"It's absolutely lovely, Richard," she crooned delightedly as she held it up for inspection. "I shall invent special occasions for wearing it."

"You're the only girl I know who could wear it."

Jane looked at him quizzically. "Your saying that reminds me. What about that girl you met just before you went away, Sarah somebody?"

"She greeted my return with roses."

Jane raised a sardonic eyebrow. "Not red ones, I hope, or you really are sunk."

"Yellow as a matter of fact."

"That's not quite so significant! And what have you brought her?"

"A fan. I've brought everyone fans, except you."

"Alan's always wanted one," she said gravely.

It was soon after this that Alan himself returned. He gave Richard a friendly pat on the shoulder before kissing his wife and daughter.

"Did you win your case, darling?" Jane inquired.

"Yes," he said with mock gravity, while Richard grinned. To Jane, all her husband's cases were gladiatorial contests in which he charged around like a knight in shining armour.

"Who were you defending?" Richard asked.

"I was prosecuting. It was a robbery case. Jury were only out ten minutes and the judge gave him seven years."

"Sounds as if it was a walk-over."

"It was. He ought to have pleaded, but old Halback defended and you know what he is for making forensic bricks without the aid of any straw."

"Makes and then drops them on the judge's toes," Richard observed.

While Jane was putting Sophie to bed, Alan and he moved into the sitting-room.

"Has Japan changed your drinking habits?" Alan asked, going across to the drink cupboard.

"Not noticeably."

"Still no spirits?"

"Not even saké."

"Sherry, then?"

"Just the job."

Alan handed Richard his drink and fetched himself a gin and tonic.

"It really is nice to see you again, Richard," he said as he sat down and stretched out comfortably. He was taller than

Richard and was good looking in a lean way. His great quality as an advocate was unflappability. Whatever unexpected twists his cases might take in court he remained imperturbable. He also had the inestimable quality of generally going down well with both judges and juries. The one liked him because he was straightforward and didn't waste time, the other because he was devoid of the more trying habits of his profession and was completely unpompous.

It was Richard who exuded restless energy and was always trying out new things from tooth-paste to motor-cars and who secretly regarded himself as a James Bond manqué—very manqué. It was Alan who was urbane and sophisticated and completely in tune with life. By all rights Alan should have been the one who lived in Mayfair and took exotic holidays abroad, but this was where reality and convention parted company.

They had been talking only a short time before Richard related his encounter with Eddie Butcher.

Alan listened with growing interest and without interrupting.

"Where was Butcher going when you parted company at the airport this morning?" he asked at the end.

"I've no idea. He didn't tell me and I didn't ask him. To be perfectly honest, after sixteen hours flying and with the clock standing on its head, I was quite happy to see the back of him."

"I doubt whether you have for long from all you've told me."

"So do I. I imagine he'll be in touch with me within a day or two."

"What do you think he'll try and do?"

"Try and do?"

"Well, obviously he hasn't come back just to settle in the country and take up market gardening. On the contrary it looks very much as if he has every intention of re-entering the lion's den. The lion being Caspar, of course. Why otherwise should he contemplate requiring your services?"

"I think he regards me in the same light as an insurance policy. It doesn't mean that your house can't be burnt down, merely that there are consolations if it is. He clearly expects Caspar to find out pretty soon that he is back in England and after that anything can happen."

Alan pursed his lips. "I suppose it's within the bounds of possibility that he won't have any opportunity of getting in touch with you. That he'll be despatched with the speed of a bullet. Caspar must be mighty sore at losing fifty thousand pounds. Apart from which you can't let your employees get away with that sort of thing. It's bad for discipline."

"Well, whatever does transpire," Richard said, "I hope you'll be ready to accept a brief."

Alan grinned. "It's certainly a case with a wide range of possibilities. It could develop in almost any direction—or in none."

"It'll develop all right," Richard said. "I know. I've met Butcher. He has as much chance of keeping out of trouble as a lump of sugar can avoid melting in a cup of coffee."

Alan's expression became thoughtful. "I suppose there's no question of Caspar having reported Butcher's defalcation to the police?"

"Absolutely none, I'd say. It would lead to their inquiring into the whole elaborate set-up of fraudulent companies, and that's a prospect he couldn't begin to face."

Alan nodded. "Yes, that must be right. But if he could get away with it, it would be a neat way of disposing of Butcher, namely to use the existing legal machinery to lodge him in prison for a few years."

"From what I've heard of Caspar, he would regard that as a totally inadequate punishment for what Butcher's done."

At this moment Jane joined them and the conversation moved away from the clouded prospects of Butcher's future.

It wasn't until the end of the evening when Alan accompanied Richard out to his car that anything further was said in the matter.

"I'll get in touch with you just as soon as I hear from Butcher," Richard said. "Or *of* him," he added after a second's pause.

6

Ralph Caspar folded the *Financial Times* neatly and laid it on the sofa beside him. He glanced at his watch and saw that it was four o'clock. Tendo and Ebony were late. They must have got held up in a traffic jam. He had phoned them over an hour ago and asked them to come round to the flat straight away. There was nothing he could do but wait with as much patience as he could muster; This, however, was not particularly difficult for him as he regarded impatience as an indication of weakness, of a lack of control, and had learnt to overcome it. He eschewed all emotion, save that deliberately exhibited for calculated effect.

He got up and walked over to the window and gazed down on the ant-like figures scurrying along the pavements below. To him, they meant no more than ants. He regarded them with indifference so long as they didn't trouble him.

The front-door buzzer sounded and he went out into the hall. He put his eye to the spy-hole to make sure that his callers were those he was expecting.

"Sorry we're late, Ralph," Tendo said. "They've ploughed up Welbeck Street overnight and you've never seen such a bloody jam."

Jack Ebony nodded as if to corroborate this statement. He was a short, dark, Italianate man with eyes which gave the appearance of missing nothing. Tony Tendo could hardly have presented a greater physical contrast, and resembled nothing so much as a Scandinavian rugger forward, if such a hybrid can be imagined.

Caspar led the way into the sitting-room and waved a hand towards the drink cabinet.

"Help yourselves."

Tendo fetched himself a Scotch and soda, but Ebony shook his head.

"We called on Pratt this morning," Ebony said and threw a wad of notes down on the table. "There's £650 there. But I suspect he's still keeping some back."

Caspar looked at the money as though it had no interest for him. "We'll go into that later," he said coldly. "I want to discuss something different. Eddie Butcher's back. I had a cable from Tokyo this morning, saying it was thought he left there the day before yesterday on a direct flight."

"Why didn't they stop him?"

"Why indeed!" Caspar said in a grim tone. "It couldn't have been very difficult to have got rid of him. However, I'll suspend judgment until I receive Fukiko's full report. Meanwhile," he went on in the same chilling tone, "Eddie has slipped back into the country and we don't know where he is."

"He may have got off en route and not yet be here," Tendo remarked.

"If you don't mind, we'll assume he is here," Caspar replied evenly.

"In that event, I reckon it won't be long before we hear from him," Ebony said. He gave the other two a smile which was no more than a curl of one end of his upper lip. "He'll be looking for the girl."

"That's for certain," Tendo agreed. "And he'll be driven to get in touch with us to find out where she is. Incidentally, Ralph, where is she?"

Caspar frowned. "All I know is that we successfully frightened her out of town once we had got from her that Eddie had made for Japan. I told her that if she crossed my path again, she'd not get off with a caution next time." He directed his frown at a well-manicured nail. "I'm reasonably satisfied that she won't set foot in London again until it's to visit her grandchildren,"

"She was scared all right at the end," Tendo said.

"She was scared at the beginning," Ebony added.

"But even more scared by the end." Tendo's tone held a note of relish.

"But that still doesn't help us to know where she is now," Caspar said judicially. "On the other hand, Eddie has no chance of getting in touch with her and there's no way by which she can find out that he's back in England. Moreover, once he fails to discover her in her old haunts, the odds are he'll suspect that I'm responsible for having spirited her away. In fact, he'll be drawn to me like a bent nail to a magnet."

"Just what I said at the start . . ." Ebony broke in.

"And there's no reason," Caspar went on, ignoring the interruption, "why I shouldn't let him think that I do know her

47

whereabouts. I might even give him the idea that I have taken her into protective custody. I could tempt him to don his shining armour and try a rescue operation . . . . No, I think we can be quite certain of a telephone call from our Eddie within the next few days."

"I suppose there's no chance of the girl having gone off to some old aunt or cousin in the country whom Eddie knows about, so that he would automatically go looking for her there?" Tendo's expression was that of a giant seeing his prey slip through the bars of the portcullis.

Caspar shook his head. "If you remember I checked on her background very carefully when Eddie first took up seriously with her. Father's dead, mother's re-married and lives in New Zealand, no brothers, no sisters, just a handful of friends in London. I'm pretty sure that Eddie knew nothing more about her than he told me." He smiled thinly, "In fact, she's the perfect victim for a disappearance act. There's nobody to ask any questions—except Eddie, and nobody to whom he can address his questions—except me." In a brisker tone, he went on, "However, I never like to feel the grass growing under my feet and so we won't just sit back and wait for Eddie to get in touch with us. I want every effort made to find him first."

Ebony and Tendo both nodded their acknowledgement of the instruction.

"Not that I imagine he'll frequent any of his known haunts," Caspar continued. "He must realise that he's running certain risks in returning. Or should I say, more certain risks! No, my guess is he'll keep right away from all his old friends."

"Nevertheless, we'll try," Ebony said.

"Yes, try . . ." Caspar replied, and his voice trailed away as a thoughtful expression took possession of his features. It was several seconds before he spoke again. When he did, it was to dismiss the matter under discussion from the agenda. He appeared to have come to a sudden decision which had cleared his mind about Butcher. "Now let's hear about Pratt," he said, turning to Ebony. "It sounds as if we may need to remind him that his bread is well buttered on the under-side and that it's preferable this way to his not being able to enjoy either butter or bread . . ."

Paula Caspar was waiting for the telephone to ring. To all intents and purposes she was alone in the house. Her sister, Eileen, was somewhere out at the back—probably getting the cats their supper. She spent apparent hours on this particular chore. Though if you stopped to think, as Paula now did, she spent hours on everything. On making the beds, on washing up, even on boiling a kettle for tea. Anyone might suppose she kept house for a dozen instead of for a maximum of three including herself and more often than not, only two, as Ralph spent a good many nights in town.

Nevertheless, it was a satisfactory arrangement. It provided Eileen with a home and Paula with a housekeeper. It wasn't that her elder sister was mentally defective, just that she was a bit strange in her manner. There was a time when the kitchens of grand houses were full of Eileens who were bullied by cooks and butlers, but whose devoted duty over a lifetime in the end imposed a measure of slavery upon those for whom they toiled. Not that Paula Caspar had anxious moments contemplating her sister's future. She didn't. It didn't even occur to her to contemplate it. Indeed, she sometimes almost forgot that Eileen was her sister, she had become so used to the relationship of mistress and servant, in which each largely minded her own business. It had come as something of a shock when the postman had recently commented that anyone would have known them for sisters. If it was true, it was certainly not something Paula cared to be reminded of.

She frowned as she now suddenly remembered that Eileen was shortly going on holiday. Off to Spain to join a coach tour of the South and later across to Morocco for a few days. Paula felt she could just picture her sister sitting placidly aloof in the hot, dusty coach while Arab urchins exhausted their energies trying to wheedle a few coins out of her. The fact remained, however, that whatever anyone might secretly think of Eileen's I.Q., she regularly went off each year alone on these foreign trips from which, with equal regularity, she safely returned, and which, so far as anyone could gather, she thoroughly enjoyed in her own arcane way.

At last the telephone rang and Paula's hand shot out to answer it.

"Is that Mrs. Caspar?" a voice inquired.

"Yes, Mrs. Caspar speaking."

"Good afternoon, Mrs. Caspar. This is Mr. Poultney."

"Yes!" Her tone was impatient. "Do you have any news for me?"

"I think I can definitely say there is another woman," Mr. Poultney replied in the conspiratorial whisper which was part of his stock-in-trade but which, had he but known it, a good many of his clients, Paula Caspar among them, found excessively tiresome.

"Yes, but who is she?" Paula snapped. "I as good as knew that there was someone before I hired you. Your job was to find out who she is."

"I know, dear lady," Mr. Poultney said, adopting his soothing tone, which could be as irritating as his conspiratorial whisper. "But this sort of assignment takes time. One has to move with caution. Impatient haste can undo everything in a matter of minutes."

"Well, when do you think you will have definite news?"

"Soon, dear lady, quite soon, I hope." He gave a nervous cough. "There is just one other little matter we could perhaps straighten out ..."

"Yes?"

"Would it be asking too much to request you to put a cheque in the post? Say, fifty pounds? I'm afraid these little inquiries do rather run away with the money, but it's work which calls for a skilled operator and that does send up the price."

"But I gave you a hundred pounds only ten days ago."

"I know you did, dear lady, and to be quite truthful I thought that would see us through, but—and I hope you won't be offended at my mentioning this—Mr. Caspar is rather out of the ordinary run of errant husband. I'm sure you understand what I mean?"

"I'm afraid I don't."

"Tch!" Mr. Poultney sounded actually embarrassed. After a pause he said, "Well, may I put it another way? This is an assignment which I feel calls for danger money. Normally, the worst that happens if one is unfortunate enough to be spotted by the suspect under surveillance is a torrent of abuse and occasionally a little bit of rough stuff, but never anything serious, and if I do happen to become cornered, I can usually give as good as I get. Though, of course, one tries to avoid anything of the sort, as confrontations of that nature can only be regarded as a mark of failure. Not that it's necessarily one's own fault. Nevertheless, one tries to avoid them for everyone's sake." He paused uncomfortably. "But your husband, if you will permit me to say so, is in rather a different category. In the first place, he is much more difficult to keep under observation than the ordinary run of husband and, in the second, the risks to the investigator's life and limb are much greater.

In the very unfortunate event, dear lady, of Mr. Caspar cottoning on to me, I don't imagine I'd be subjected to mere abuse or even a healthy black eye . . . I'm sure you see what I mean . . ."

Paula Caspar saw very clearly what he meant. "Very well, I'll send you a further fifty pounds," she said briskly, "but I hope to have full results soon."

"Oh you will, dear lady, rest assured of that, I'm giving this matter my most earnest personal attention. I certainly trust that I shall be able to report 'assignment completed' within the next week or ten days. I had hoped to be able to do so before now, but Mr. Caspar, in addition to everything else, is discreet, almost to the point of being elusive in pursuit of his little infidelity. Add to that, the extra precautions required . . ."

"Yes, yes, I understand all that," Paula Caspar broke in impatiently. Mr. Poultney had made his point and she had accepted it. There was no need for him to go on trying to impress her with what she already knew, namely her husband's power and cunning. She had been married to him for twelve years, which was ample time to have discovered that. Not that she had any regrets about her marriage. It had been as successful as she had ever expected it to be. More so, perhaps. Even now, Ralph Caspar was nothing less than correct in his attitude toward her.

Paula was twenty-four when he plucked her out of the bar of a small Soho night club and married her. She was not a girl who had expected to marry for love, and so this aspect of their life together brought her no worry. She was his second wife and, if anyone had asked her at the time, would have shrugged off as irrelevant whether she was likely to be his last. In short, she was a hard, calculating bitch who, nevertheless, realised that self-interest, if nothing else, often required the exercise of a measure of compromise.

She had known for some time that her husband was being unfaithful, but it was only recently she had become bored with the situation and had decided that this might be turned to her future advantage. Consequently, her first step had been to try and find out with whom he was having an affair, and this was where Mr. Poultney came in. He had been recommended to her by a friend who had employed him in similar circumstances.

Amongst other characteristics, Paula and her husband shared the same degree of cool self-control. Moreover, so far as he was concerned, she had the virtue of not asking questions, of not wanting to play any part in his activities other than enjoy the proceeds. In the first instance, he had married her entirely for her looks and for her performance between the sheets. Later he had come to respect her almost masculine detachment in reaching judgments, but even then only in his own detached way.

Jack Ebony had once described them as being like a couple of show cats.

It was about five minutes after Paula had finished talking to Mr. Poultney that the telephone rang again. She lifted the receiver and immediately heard her husband's voice.

" 'Fraid I shan't get home tonight, Paula."

"Where are you staying?"

"At the flat, of course. Where else?"

"I thought you might be going off somewhere."

"No, I'll be at the flat if you want me. What'll you do?"

"I might go to the cinema. I might just stay in and watch television."

"Enjoy yourself whichever you do," he said in a tone which he might have used to bid a stranger "good night". "There is just one thing I ought to mention. Eddie Butcher might telephone. Tell him I'm at the flat."

"I thought you told me he was abroad."

"He's come back."

"O.K. I'll tell him if he does ring."

"Thanks, pet. See you tomorrow evening. 'Night."

"Good-night, Ralph."

She had met Butcher several times and rather liked him. The one she couldn't stand was Tony Tendo. To her, he was just a hunk of not very attractive meat. But his wife Bridget seemed to find him all right, and she was a bright enough girl. It just showed how everyone's glands functioned differently.

She yawned and got up from the sofa, and went over to the french windows which looked out on the too-perfect garden, which had been laid down like a Chinese carpet at a cost of £5,000. And that hadn't included the swimming pool, which had cost a further £2,000. Instant gardens could be got these days as easily as cups of instant coffee, provided you had the money.

Not that she was interested in the garden other than somewhere to sit out in seclusion when the weather was right. She neither knew one flower from the next nor wanted to.

Round the corner out of sight was her car. A red T.R.4 with black leather uholstery. She was a good driver and had taken great pride in passing her advanced driving test. She liked nothing better than to get behind the wheel, and would experience a sensual pleasure in the co-ordination of all the mental and physical reflexes required in a piece of expert driving.

Tomorrow would provide such an occasion when she drove down to the village near Wantage where Aeolus was stabled. He was a two-year-old she had bought at one of the lesser sales the previous autumn and on whom she had since lavished an intense interest. Becoming a registered race-horse owner had given her even greater satisfaction than passing the advanced driving test, and to see a jockey actually wearing her colours was still the biggest thrill of all.

She had entered this new world, knowing nothing about it but with determination to establish herself as quickly as possible. If there was one thing which couldn't be said against Paula Caspar it was that she had the attributes of a dilettante. Whatever she gave her mind to, she gave it wholeheartedly—whether it was acquiring a better position in life, driving a car or owning a racehorse.

She heard the door open behind her and looked round. It was her sister Eileen.

"Is Ralph coming home for dinner tonight?" she asked in the oddly incurious tone in which she spoke.

"No, he phoned just now to say he wouldn't be. I can manage if you want to go out."

"I'll probably go down to bingo then."

"It's time you won another prize."

"You can come with me if you like."

"Me? Bingo? All those old crones gloating over their boards. No thank you!"

Eileen said nothing, nor was it possible to tell from her expression whether she accepted or repudiated this description of her evening's activities. She just went on standing inside the door looking unconcerned.

"I can cook you something before I go. It doesn't start till eight," she said at length.

"All right, we can have an early snack together. I don't want much."

"Do you think you'll manage all right while I'm away?" she asked in the same incurious tone.

"I always have done. Anyway, Mrs. Goode will still be coming in. What time do you actually leave next Thursday?"

"It's a night flight." She came a bit further into the room and said suddenly, "Do you ever get worried about Ralph, Paula?"

"What on earth do you mean?" Paula Caspar's tone was sharper than she'd meant, but the question had taken her by surprise.

"I mean, do you ever get worried about losing all this?" Her glance went round the comfortable furnished room, and she made a vague gesture in the direction of the garden. "Aren't you ever nervous that the police will get on to Ralph?"

"I'm sure Ralph is well able to look after his affairs," Paula replied coldly. "He's a good deal smarter than the police." She had no intention of telling her sister that she had made sure she would be properly provided for in the event of anything going badly wrong.

"Don't think I'm worrying for myself!" Eileen added.

"Well, that's fine then," Paula said crisply. "And you certainly don't have to worry for me." She fixed her sister with a severe look. "I hope you never give Ralph any idea of the sort of thoughts you've just been expressing, because he wouldn't like it a bit. I've told you before, he doesn't welcome any interference in his activities—and that goes for idle speculation, too."

Eileen's only response was to give her a dreamy look before departing from the room.

Paula decided that she had been tried sufficiently for one afternoon and went upstairs to have a bath.

7

Eddie Butcher had gone straight from the airport to a small hotel off Gloucester Road where he had taken a room under an assumed name. It was not a district of London with which he had been associated and he felt it would be a safe base for operations. It was certainly well away from any of Caspar's fields of activity. Not that this meant he proposed running any risks. On the contrary, he had from the first moment of stepping off the plane acted on the assumption that danger lay hidden at every point of the compass. Not least danger in the guise of monstrous coincidence. The sort which would bring Caspar strolling for the first time in his life down the road in which the hotel lay and right past the door just as Butcher came past.

As soon as he had booked in, he made a series of telephone calls to try and trace Diane.

At the place where she had worked a strange voice said, "Diane Paisley? Used to work here, you say . . . Hang on, I'll ask someone . . . I gather she left two or three months ago . . . No, sorry, nobody's heard anything from her since she went . . . Good-bye."

He next phoned the flat in Fulham which she had shared with three other girls, but there was no answer. It could only be that they had all left for work. Luckily, he was able to recall that one of them, Mary Thomson, worked as secretary to the manager of a branch of Thos. Cook.

"Mary, this is Eddie Butcher," he said, aware of a sudden contriction of his throat as he heard her voice and realised how much her answer meant to him. "Do you know how I can get hold of Diane?"

"Did you say Eddie Butcher?"

"Yes, remember, we met a couple of times through Diane?"

"I thought you'd gone to live abroad."

"I've just come back."

"Well, I'm afraid I can't help you over Diane." Her tone was unfriendly.

"Look, Mary, it's terribly important that I get in touch with her. Do you mean you can't or you won't help me?"

"I mean that I can't. I don't know where she is."

"When did you last see her?"

"About a week after she said you'd left."

"What happened then? Where'd she go?" he asked urgently.

"I don't know where she went. She just packed up and left in a hurry. In a very considerable hurry. It was obvious that she was scared stiff. One might almost say she was rigid with fright about something, but she refused to tell me what it was. Said she didn't want anyone else involved and it was better that she got out quickly."

Eddie swallowed, but his throat felt as though something the size of a golf ball was stuck painfully half way down.

"Didn't she say at all where she was going?" he asked desperately.

"No." Her tone throbbed with pent-up reproach like a boil ready for lancing.

Eddie groaned. "I've got to find her somehow! Do you know whether she left alone or whether someone fetched her."

"I can't tell you that either. She was there when I left for work one morning and gone when I got back in the evening. There was just a note saying she wouldn't be coming back, and with it some money settling up her share of things."

"And that was the last you heard of her?"

"Yes."

Though he had met Mary, he gathered that Diane had never given her any clue as to what he did for a living. Mary presumably thought that they had broken up as a result of a lover's quarrel, though she must have wondered, and indeed still be wondering, what it was that had sent Diane into petrified flight. He must try and put this straight.

Diffidently he said, "I haven't been in touch with Diane since I left. I promise you I didn't have anything to do with frightening her away."

"Someone did," Mary replied remorselessly.

Yes, someone did all right! Moreover, he knew who that someone was.

After speaking to Mary Thomson, he made calls to two acquaintances of Diane's who, he thought, might have had news of her. He rang, however, without much hope, and his pessimism was justified by the negative result.

He spent the rest of the day drifting from one coffee bar to the next, with interludes in public houses when they were open.

By eleven o'clock that night, when he returned to his hotel, his thoughts had still failed to break out of the squirrel cage in which they had been claustrophobically rotating the whole day.

Somehow he had to find Diane! For the first time in his life he had acted out of feeling for another person. He had retraced his steps from the opposite side of the world all on account of a girl, only to discover that she had vanished. Vanished, moreover, in circumstances to arouse anxieties such as he had never experienced before. He had several times in his life been frightened for his own skin, but this was worse by far because of his impotence to confront the reality of the situation. It was like shadow boxing in the echoing vaults of hell. All day long he had wrestled with his thoughts trying to re-arrange them like pieces of a jig-saw puzzle. But the trouble with a jig-saw puzzle is that the pieces will only make one picture, however hard you try otherwise.

By the time he returned to the hotel that evening he knew, as he had known since morning, that there was only one person left whom he could approach. It was that or creeping away and losing himself as though he had never returned.

Full of anxiety and foreboding, but now firmly resolved, he climbed into bed and lay for a further hour in rigid wakefulness.

At nine o'clock the next morning he took the underground to Victoria Station, shut himself into a public telephone box and dialled the number of Caspar's flat.

There was a moment of cold panic when he heard the well-known answer, and he had to force his hand to push home the coins.

'Hello, Ralph. This is Eddie." He could picture the unruffled reception of this announcement at the other end. Caspar showed no more emotion in directing that someone should be liquidated than in ordering a plate of sardines on toast.

"I had heard you were back, Eddie. I was telling Paula only last night that you might ring. How did you find Japan?"

"You know why I'm calling you, Ralph?"

"Maybe I do, maybe I don't, so you tell me."

"I want to know where Diane is."

"I see! And what makes you think I can help you to find her?"

"Look, Ralph, shall we cut out all the fencing! I know that she's disappeared and I know you're responsible. And I want to know where she is."

"And what can you offer me in exchange?"

"Nothing, unless you have any reasonable suggestions."

"That, at least, has the merit of frankness. It also shows a fair amount of impudence. However, I see no reason why we shouldn't attempt to negotiate, even though you do sound like the man in a buyer's market without a bean in his pocket. Anyway, let us see where we get."

"You're crazy if you think I'm going to agree to meet you."

"That, of course, is up to you. If you don't want to meet me, I might as well hang up." There was a silence, then Caspar said, "Look, Eddie, I'll be frank with you. I won't pretend that you're my favourite person at the moment. I feel much the same as any other guy who's been chiselled out of fifty thousand pounds. Believe me, it's a disagreeable sensation. Nevertheless, I'm pleased to think that I'm a sufficiently objective-minded person to recognise audacious planning and slick execution when I see them. And not only recognise, but make use of them, even when they've been turned against me. What I'm saying is that I'm ready to discuss a further business arrangement with you."

"What about the fifty thousand pounds?"

"There's no reason why that can't somehow be incorporated in our deal. That is, if we come to a deal. I'm not committing myself in advance."

"And supposing we don't reach a deal? what then?"

"We'll jump that hurdle when we get to it."

"How do I know this isn't a trap?"

"A very reasonable question. I've been thinking while we've been talking. Supposing I suggest a rendezvous which you can reach and leave without anyone knowing you've been there. Supposing I'm also able to satisfy you that I shall be absolutely alone: that Tony and Jack will be miles away and that we can talk alone, after which you can fade away in the night. Supposing I can arrange all that, what would your answer be?"

Eddie felt the sweat pouring off him. And it wasn't only the heat in the call box which was causing it. He threw a wild-eyed glance through the glass panel of the door and was met by one of ill-suppressed irritation from a young man waiting to make a call.

"I'm ready to listen," he said cautiously, turning his back firmly on the door and focussing his whole attention on the receiver as though it had oracular propensities.

"Fine. Then this is what I suggest . . ."

8

Richard had been back in the office three days and still hadn't had a call from Eddie Butcher. He had somehow expected to have had him on the phone several times a day and though the continuing silence didn't arouse any special anxieties in him, he was puzzled. But then he would reflect how a change of scene invariably also brings a change of perspective and with a shrug he would concentrate his mind on the backlog of work which was awaiting his attention.

Nevertheless he found Eddie intruding on his thoughts whenever they were not fully occupied with something else, and sometimes when they were. He realised that events in Japan had forged a bond of sorts between them. His interest, his curiosity, indeed all his instincts as a criminal lawyer, had been brought into play. He felt like a car engine which had been warmed up for the race, only to be switched off and left to cool.

As the end of Friday approached, he even began to wonder if he would ever hear anything further of Eddie. But that was a disturbing thought, since it wouldn't necessarily mean that Eddie hadn't tried to get in touch with him. From all he had heard, quite a few people had vanished without trace at a snap of Caspar's fingers. And in Eddie's case, there was no one apart from Richard to ask any awkward questions.

He got up from behind his mahogany desk with its dark green leather top and walked across to one of the two windows which stretched down to the floor and gave on to a small wrought-iron veranda of dubious safety. He looked out with appreciation on the elegant façade of Bedford Square. Some of the people who worked there might have preferred less external elegance and greater internal comfort, including, probably, one or two of his own junior clerks who were housed at the top of the building in rooms which couldn't be cooled in summer or heated in winter and whose floors undulated in a disquieting way.

Richard's own room, however mirrored the external elegance in every way. It was newly carpeted in a green which matched the top of his desk, on which stood a brass table lamp. On one wall there were four Spy cartoons with their legal flavour of another period. Against the whole length of another ran bookshelves which stretched from floor to ceiling and which contained bound volumes of the Law Reports, a large number of text-books and the collected "famous trials" series. At one end of a middle shelf were half a dozen fat red leather diaries with the year of use in gold letters on the spine. These were Richard's personal diaries in which he recorded the details of his own cases. He had them specially bound and they were filled with his small, neat handwriting. Such corrections and additions as there were were hardly less neat than the original text.

Sheila Gillam came through the door which divided their two rooms.

"Anything else you'll be wanting this evening, Mr. Monk?"

"No thanks, Sheila." He cast a moody glance at the stack of folders at one side of his desk. "I hope I shall feel more like work on Monday."

"There's not much backlog left," she said comfortingly. "You've done pretty well these three days you've been back."

"It hasn't felt like it."

"I don't see how you could expect otherwise. I find it hard enough settling down again after a long weekend in the Cotswolds. I believe the person who comes bursting back to work full of eager zest is a myth. What's more . . ." She broke off and began to blush as it suddenly occurred to her that her employer was normally such a mythical person. "Is that my phone ringing?" She darted back into her room, but re-appeared a moment later. "Your Mr. Butcher has never rung," she remarked, hoping to cover up her gaffe. Not that she stood in any fear of Richard. On the contrary it was the desire to avoid hurting him rather than fear of arousing his temper which motivated her. She enjoyed working for him enormously and found him as near the perfect boss as she could imagine. As a married girl there was a great advantage in not having a boss who was constantly making passes.

"No, he hasn't," Richard replied in an abstracted tone.

Sheila frowned. She realised that he was bothered by the fact, and that there was absolutely nothing she could do to help. But good secretary as she was she suffered vicariously with him for a few seconds; then her practical side reasserted itself, and with a small shrug, she bade him a pleasant weekend and returned to her own room where she picked up her belongings and left.

Turning back to the window, he watched her until she passed from sight round the corner. Good secretary, good wife—and that was as well, seeing that her husband Harold was a struggling actor whose barometric moods could hit all-time lows of depression.

He went back to his desk and sat down. For another hour he worked his way through files, more on the off chance that the telephone might yet go than of wanting to get something finished.

But the telephone didn't ring and at half-past six he left and walked home.

"Hi, Bridge, I'm back," Tony Tendo called out cheerfully as he slammed the front-door of his home behind him that same Friday evening.

Bridget Tendo who was in the living-room watching the end of a television programme, permitted herself a resigned flicker of a frown. She hated being called Bridge. It was worse than Bridget and that was bad enough. Why did her parents have to give her such a primly awful name! Why did a devoted husband have to make it sound stupider than it was!

He came into the room and bent over the chair to kiss her warmly.

"I've got news, Bridge, we're going down to Brighton for the weekend." He stood back and looked at her with approving pleasure. "Say you're happy."

She smiled back at him. The smile of a mother who is happy when her child is happy. It was absurd how protective she could feel toward this man who could lift her with one hand and make her feel like a doll in the hug of a great bear.

"Of course I'm happy, Tony. When are we off?"

"As soon as you're ready."

"But what's all this about?" she asked as she stood up.

"Just that Ralph thought he might want Jack and me tomorrow and now he doesn't. It was he who insisted we should go away for the weekend. He even phoned the hotel and made the reservations himself. If we go now, we can have a late meal when we arrive and then go dancing. Brighton has some nice spots. I thought we'd try that club we saw last time but didn't go to."

"Are Jack and Marie coming too?"

"Yea, we'll meet them down there. Go and pack that new sexy nightdress I bought you and we'll be off."

"Seen the evening paper, Tony?" she inquired as she made to leave the room.

"Who wants newspapers tonight!"

"There's an item on one of the middle pages you can read while I'm getting ready."

"Tell me first what it's about?" he said, as he went across to the small bar, which occupied one corner of the room, and poured himself a large Scotch. The bar was his special pride and he always switched on the ship's port and starboard lights, which hung at either end, as soon as he came into the room.

"It's about Ronald Pratt."

"Oh, Ronnie Pratt! What's it say?"

"That he'd met with a sort of accident."

"Yea, I heard that, too," he said with a knowing wink.

"It said also that he had been unable to assist the police in identifying his assailants."

"Well that shows he still has a bit of sense left."

Bridget Tendo shivered as though the temperature of the room had suddenly dropped.

"You run such terrible risks, Tony, sometimes I get scared."

He came across and put an arm round her shoulder, pulling her into his side.

"You don't have to worry about me, Bridge," he said gently, "Mine's a job like anyone else's except it pays a bit better." With a note of self-satisfaction, he went on. "Nobody squeals when Jack and I hurt them because they know what'll happen if they do. They know it's far healthier to keep in with us than it is with the police."

She scanned his expression, to realise not for the first time that his chief qualification for his job, apart from physical strength, was his lack of imagination. An intelligence which weighed up all the risks could only have been a disadvantage.

He gave her a fond smack on the behind. "Now, go and get our things together, Bridge."

As she walked about the bedroom pulling things out of drawers and cupboards and putting them into a small suitcase, she hummed thoughtfully beneath her breath.

Downstairs, her husband poured himself another Scotch and sat down opposite the bar which he never tired of staring at.

He didn't reckon they'd have any further trouble from

Ronnie Pratt. They'd given him a thorough going-over before dumping him battered and terrified half a mile from his home.

Though that was nothing to the treatment waiting to be meted out to Eddie Butcher, once they found *him*.

9

Richard had invited Sarah Wyatt round for a drink that evening with the idea that they might afterwards go and see a film.

However, what with his getting back only a few minutes before she arrived, coupled with the strength of the martinis he mixed and, he subsequently suspected, Sarah's steady determination to keep the evening quiet and cosy, they stayed in and ate scrambled eggs, followed by Camembert cheese, with which they polished off a bottle of Moselle.

Later, they just sat and talked. And as the talk ran down he put an arm round her shoulder and pulled her warm, yielding body against his. He kissed her and time went by, so that it was after midnight when he drove her home. He was still uncertain, at the end of the evening, exactly what his feelings were toward her. She was pretty, she was amusing without being wildly intellectual, but she somehow made it a bit too obvious that she regarded him as worthy prey. He was not to know that she entertained a number of reservations about himself. At the risk of being unflattered, he might have felt rather easier in his mind if he had.

It was about a quarter past one when he switched out his bedside light and immediately dropped off to sleep.

He had no idea how long he'd been asleep when the telephone bell burst into his dreams like a hundred fire engines. He put out a feverish hand for the receiver. Anything to stop the shattering din.

"Mr. Monk? This is Eddie Butcher." His voice did nothing to lessen the tension. Indeed, Richard experienced an almost physical dread of what might follow. Still holding the receiver to his ear, he managed to switch on the light. The clock on his bedside table showed two-fifteen.

"Mr. Monk, may I come to your flat straight away? Something's happened."

"O.K., come along," Richard replied in a tone which was as taut as a piano wire. "Where are you now?"

"Near the Kingston by-pass. I'll be with you in about twenty minutes."

"You know my address?"

"Yes."

After Butcher had rung off, Richard got up and went into the kitchen to put on some coffee. Then he cleaned his teeth, combed his hair and retired to the living-room to await his visitor's arrival.

It was the longest twenty minutes he could ever remember, and, although listening till his ears ached, he jumped nervously when eventually there was a short, sharp buzz at the front door.

Eddie stepped swiftly inside as soon as the door was opened. He was wearing the same dark blue jacket with silver buttons and the fawn trousers which he had worn the evening of their first meeting at the hotel near Mount Fuji just under two weeks ago. His hair was slightly dishevelled and he had a pallor which showed up against his shaving line like a photographic negative.

Richard closed the door and instinctively put it on the chain.

"Come into the sitting-room." He motioned Eddie along the passage toward the lighted room. "You look as though you could do with a drink! There's coffee ready, but perhaps you'd prefer something stronger."

Eddie nodded. "Whisky if you've got it," he said in a hoarse voice.

Richard poured him a treble and went and fetched the coffee for himself. By the time he returned, Eddie's glass was empty and some of the tension seemed to have left him. He accepted Richard's unspoken invitation to a refill.

"And now," Richard said, handing him back his glass, "you'd better tell me what's happened."

Eddie shook his head as though to clear it of muzziness. "I think," he said with almost painful effort, "that I've walked straight into Caspar's trap. Straight bloody in!" He looked directly at Richard. "To think . . . to think I could have been so blind, except that I wasn't all that blind. I was put off by his change of tactics. It wasn't that I trusted him, but I thought I could handle the situation. I realise now that he led me to think so . . ." He shook his head in further anguish. "I'm sorry, Mr. Monk. I'm afraid I'm not being very clear. But it's a relief just to be talking aloud. If you give me a moment, I'll try and tell you the whole story in proper order." He took a gulp of his drink, fixed Richard with a steady look and said, "The

66

long and short of it is, Mr. Monk, that I'm fairly certain I've been framed for a murder."

"Whose murder?"

"Paula Caspar's. Tonight. Someone murdered her all right. Shot her through the back of the head.

"Now start at the beginning," Richard said, leaning forward and clasping his mug of coffee like a hand-warmer.

"Ever since I got back. I've been trying to find Diane, but I've drawn a succession of blanks. The more inquiries I made, the more certain I became that Caspar knew what had happened to her . . ."

"You don't mean . . .?"

"I don't know what I mean. Only that she's disappeared and nobody knows where she is. That is, nobody except Caspar. If he's harmed her, I'll . . . I'll . . . I'm sorry, Mr. Monk, I'll try and stick to what's happened. As I was saying, I reached the stage where I had to approach Caspar or do nothing. So I phoned him. It was immediately obvious he knew what had happened to Diane and after a good deal of fencing around he suggested we should meet and have a discussion."

"Didn't that alert you?"

"Alert me! It rang every alarm bell in my system. But that's where he was clever. He first of all made out that, by putting one over on him the way I did, I had shown myself smarter than he'd thought I was, and he'd like to talk about our doing further business together. I said I only wanted to find out where Diane was and it was then he suggested a meeting which might satisfy us both. The point was that he didn't overdo his part. He didn't pretend that I was the prodigal son returned. He made it sound simply that we might be able to reach a bargain. He obviously realised that I suspected a trap, because it was then that he proposed a meeting down at his home near Weybridge this evening. He said that there'd be only him and me. He said he'd tell Tendo and Ebony to go away for the weekend and that I could phone them at a hotel in Brighton at ten o'clock to make sure they were really there."

"And did you?"

"Yes, from a call box in Weybridge. And they were there."

"You spoke to each of them?"

"Yes."

"And they knew it was you phoning?"

"No. Caspar said he wouldn't tell them anything except that they were to be at their hotel at ten o'clock as he might want to call them himself."

"Who did you say you were?"

"I didn't. I disguised my voice. I spoke to Tony Tendo first, and when I recognised his voice, I pretended that it was Jack Ebony I'd wanted to speak to. And then he came on the line and I recognised his voice, too."

Richard nodded. "What happened after you'd rung Brighton?"

"I went straight to Caspar's house."

"Car?"

"I'd hired a mini."

"Where is it now?"

"Down the street."

Richard pursed his lips. "And then?"

"I parked it about a quarter of a mile away from Caspar's place and went the rest of the way on foot. The arrangement was that I should avoid the main entrance and skirt round the edge of the lawn until I was opposite the french window of Caspar's study."

"You knew which that was?"

"Yes. I've been to the house a number of times."

"I'm sorry. Go on."

"As I was saying, Caspar told me to come to the study french window and he'd let me in and we could talk in absolute privacy. He said that way it wouldn't matter if his wife or anyone else was in the house as they wouldn't know I had been there. He made a great point of saying that we'd be meeting on the level and in absolute secrecy." Eddie paused and looked at Richard as if to try and read his expression. "Look, Mr. Monk, put yourself in my place," he went on, with a note of urgent plea in his voice. "Caspar has the key to my finding out what's happened to Diane; he's ready to meet me and talk business; I realise there are risks but I take all the precautions open to me. In the circumstances what more could I have done?"

Eyes resting on Richard, he waited for him to answer.

"Given the overriding fact that you wanted to find out about your girlfriend, you probably did take all the precautions open to you. But a safe conduct from Caspar is, from what you've told me before, something of doubtful value. However—"

"Mr. Monk," Eddie broke in vehemently. "if the girl you love is trapped in a fire, you don't run off looking for a suit of asbestos before you dash in to rescue her. Does that explain it better?"

Richard gave a small comprehending smile. "It puts it very well. Anyway, what happened when you reached the french window?"

"There was a curtain drawn across, but I could see there was a light on in the room and I realised that the window was ajar. Or rather it was shut, but it opened slightly as I was running my hands over it. Anyway, I pushed it further open and half stepped inside. It was then I saw Paula Caspar. She was sitting in an arm-chair, one of those with a high back, and she was slumped sideways. There was blood all over the place and one of her arms, the right, was dangling over the edge of the chair. It didn't need a genius to tell she was dead."

"You said a little while ago that she'd been shot through the back of the head. How were you able to tell that?"

"There was a bullet hole in the back of the chair at head level and you could tell it passed right through her head. Her face was an awful blood-stained mess where it had come out."

"What was the lighting in the room?"

'There was just a table lamp over in one corner. It had one of those heavy shades and most of the room was in shadow, though you could see what was what well enough."

"How long did you remain in the room?"

"Just long enough to size the situation up, and not a second longer."

"Did you hear anyone in the house while you were there?"

"The only sound was my own breathing."

"And then you left the same way you'd come?"

"Yes."

"Leave any fingerprints anywhere?"

"I don't know. I gave the window a bit of a wipe, but I didn't stop to make a proper job of it. I just rubbed over where I thought I'd touched."

"I don't think you've mentioned it, what time did you get there?"

"Half past ten. That was the time Caspar told me to be there."

"And how long were you in the study altogether? Two minutes? Three minutes? Ten minutes?"

"Can't have been much more than a couple of minutes, if as much."

"Hmm." Richard appeared thoughtful. "What were you doing between, say, a quarter to eleven when you got back to where you'd parked your car and a quarter past two when you telephoned me?"

"I'd driven about five miles when I had a puncture. I had hell's own job in changing the wheel and then I found the spare wheel needed air, and it must have been over an hour before I was on the move again. I stopped at a call-box at the Esher end of the Kingston by-pass and tried to call you from there, but I couldn't get any answer."

"I was out just after midnight for about three quarters of an hour."

"I thought you might have gone away for the weekend . . . Anyway, I drove on a bit and then I stopped at an all-night café to try and sort out my thoughts. I'd more or less made up my mind then that there was no point in ringing you again before morning. However, the more I thought things over, the more desperate I became and so I decided to have another shot at getting through and that time I was successful." He was silent for a time, then said ruefully, "When we parted company at Heathrow the other morning, I didn't think our next meeting would be quite like this."

"On the other hand, you certainly envisaged trouble with Caspar," Richard reminded him.

"Not this kind of trouble!"

"To start with, you're not yet in any trouble. It's just conceivable that this wasn't a trap. It's just conceivable that it was a fortuitous event on which you stumbled."

"Do you really believe that?"

"It's a possibility. I won't say it's more than that."

Eddie shook his head. "It's not nearly such a strong possibility as my being framed for Paula Caspar's murder."

"Her husband being the actual murderer?"

"Sure! Who else?"

Another silence fell. Richard wasn't so much sleepy as aware that his reserves of mental energy were depleted. At three o'clock in the morning, the brain's batteries are apt to be running low on juice.

It was at this moment that Eddie asked, "What am I to do, Mr. Monk?"

Richard blinked. This was not the moment to stare dully at his client, and blinking at least showed that he was still alive.

"Where have you been staying?" he asked.

"The Greenway Hotel, near Gloucester Road. I'm booked in under the name of Roy Smith."

"Does anyone know you're there?"

Eddie shook his head.

"In that event, if Caspar does put the police on to you, all they can do is to issue your description and tell the world that you're someone who they believe can help them in their inquiries. But, as I say, that all depends on whether Caspar points a finger in your direction."

"He will. Having set the trap and had me walk in, he'll tell the police about me all right."

"Well, if he does and the police circulate your description, we'll make an appointment to see them."

"But what'll we tell them, Mr. Monk? That's the question, what are we going to tell them?"

"That will depend on what they ask," Richard replied with another blink. "And what they ask will depend on what they know, and what they know will depend on what they've found out."

"And what they've found out will depend on what Caspar's told them," Eddie interjected.

"To a large extent maybe, but not entirely." Richard hoisted himself out of his chair. "I suggest you now go and spend what's left of the night at your hotel, *Mr. Smith*. We'll be in touch with each other in the course of the morning, but there's nothing more we can do at the moment."

Eddie rose. "God, what a mess," he groaned. "And worst of all I'm no nearer finding out what's happened to Diane."

He looked to be near breaking point, and Richard felt like suggesting that he should stop the night in the flat, but realised that a subsequent disclosure of his could prove inhibiting if it came to defending him on a charge of murder.

If! The next few hours would almost certainly see this question resolved. After seeing Eddie out, Richard went back to bed, but lay awake in the claustrophobic darkness of his room, wondering what was happening in the big house down near Weybridge. Was it a scene of compulsive C.I.D. activity? Or did Paula Caspar still lie dead in the chair in the study undiscovered—or at any rate unreported?

10

For once in his life, Detective Inspector Drew had felt quite nonplussed, almost to the point of unsureness, but then a natural wry resilience had come to his rescue and he had, with a mental shrug, tackled the job as though it had been any other.

Nevertheless these were the last circumstances in which he had ever expected to find himself at Ralph Caspar's house. Ever since this tycoon of crime had moved into the district, D/I Drew and his men had kept a close—very close—eye on his comings and goings. The Yard Flying Squad, the Fraud Squad and the Regional Crime Squad had all taken the trouble to impress the local D/I with their interest in Caspar, but so far as the locals were concerned he had behaved impeccably. He hadn't even parked his car in a forbidden place. What went on behind the high wall which hid "Woodlands" from public view might well be a different matter, but D/I Drew had never been afforded the opportunity of finding out. To his regret. That is, until now.

He had been in bed and asleep about forty minutes when the phone had rung and Detective-Sergeant Curtis had said cheerfully, "Sorry to disturb you, sir, but we've got a murder on our hands."

Years of practice had made him immediately alert. "Do we know who it is?"

"Mrs. Caspar."

"Ralph Caspar's wife, you mean?" he had said incredulously.

"That's right, sir. Shot through the back of the head. Found by her husband."

"When?"

"About ten minutes ago, sir."

"O.K., come and pick me up and I'll be ready by the time you get here. Is anyone going ahead?"

"Yes, a patrol car should be there about now."

"I thought it was too good me getting into bed before midnight," he said with a sigh to his wife as he returned upstairs

72

to the bedroom and begun putting his clothes back on. "At least my shirt's still warm."

"What is it, a g.b.h.?" Mrs. Drew had inquired with the experience of a police officer's wife of twenty years standing.

"A murder, Caspar's wife."

"Shouldn't think you'll need to look further than her husband there."

"That's right, sew it all up for me before I even arrive on the scene," he'd replied good-humouredly. He had come round her side of the bed. "Good night, sweetheart. You can expect me for breakfast if I'm lucky." He bent down and kissed her, "But I'll have to be lucky."

And now here he was in the study of "Woodlands", staring not at the dead body of Paula Caspar but at her apparently stunned husband who was sitting in a far corner of the room holding his head in his hands and gazing at the floor as though his fate was written there.

The room seemed overcrowded and an atmosphere of orderly disorder prevailed. The photographer and the fingerprint officer were both busily engaged, while Sergeant Curtis and Detective Constable Bowen moved in and out of the study on their individual quests. Outside the study window, the ground was being examined in the patrol car's headlights.

"Is there another room we can go and talk in, Mr. Caspar?" Inspector Drew said. It was then that he first felt nonplussed, deferentially calling this elusive quarry *Mr*. Caspar as though he was one of the rich city nobs of the district, instead of someone he'd been wanting to clap inside at the first blink of an opportunity. It had remained his secret hope, despite the absence of any promise of fulfillment, that this honour would fall to him ever since Caspar moved into "Woodlands". Though he had always recognised that the Met were likely to scoop this particular pool, if anyone was. But now, by a perverted twist of fate, the man he'd been wanting to catch was enlisting his help in a murder inquiry. It was enough to nonplus the Chief Constables' Conference.

Caspar rose. "Yes, the drawing-room," he said wearily.

Inspector Drew followed him across the hall into the other room. Caspar put out a hand as they entered and flicked down the switches. To Drew's surprise a chandelier burst startlingly into light like an elaborate firework. Caspar waved him towards a chair which looked much too beautiful to be sat on. Indeed, to Drew the whole room resembled something out of a fabric designer's studio. Caspar himself sat down on the edge of a sofa as though he felt similarly inhibited. Drew noticed the neat, tidy movements with which, even in this moment of stress, he gave his trouser legs a small adjusting pull and made sure that his shirt cuffs protruded just the right amount. Only a weary greyness about his face indicated that he was under strain. The eyes were expressionless when they came up and met Drew's.

"What do you want to know, Inspector?" The tone was neither friendly nor hostile but a trifle wary. It suddenly occurred to Drew that Caspar might be experiencing the same sort of unsureness as himself in the handling of this improbable encounter.

"Were you the person who found the body?"

"Yes."

"What time was that?"

"Near enough midnight."

"Where had you been before that?"

"In London. I drove straight down. It doesn't take above forty minutes at that hour, and I left the West End about eleven fifteen."

"Where had you been in the West End?"

"At our flat, which is off Baker Street."

"I'd like you to tell me what happeened when you got back?"

"I put my car away in the garage and came in through the front door. The place was in darkness downstairs and I assumed my wife had gone up to bed. Anyway, I was about to go up myself when I noticed light coming from under the study door and went in." He passed his tongue across his lips. "My wife was slumped dead in the chair in the position you saw her."

"What did you do then?"

"Gave myself a double brandy and phoned your people."

Was it his imagination or did Drew detect a faint note of contempt when he said "your people"? Also, there was no reason why he shouldn't have had a double brandy in the circumstances—in fact, it was what most people might have prescribed for themselves—but there was something in his tone which made Drew realise what he already knew; namely, that the man was a ruthless bastard.

"So you phoned within, say, five minutes of arriving back and finding your wife dead?"

"That's about it."

"Can you think of anyone who had a motive for murdering

your wife?"

"No."

"So you can't help on that?"

"I might be able to."

"I thought you said 'no' to my question?"

"I did and I meant 'no'. I can't think of anyone who wanted to kill my wife. On the other hand, I can think of someone who wanted to kill me."

"I'm not following you."

"I'll explain—and you'd better take this down."

"I'll take a full statement from you when we've covered the ground orally. That way we shan't waste time recording irrelevances."

Armed neutrality could best describe the atmosphere engendered by this exchange. Caspar shrugged.

"I had an appointment here this evening with a man named Butcher, Eddie Butcher. We were due to meet at half past ten, but I had to go up to London about seven o'clock, and as I had no way of getting in touch with Butcher, I told my wife of the arrangement and asked her to see him and explain."

"Who is this man, Butcher?"

"Until a couple of months ago, he was a business associate of mine."

"A fellow crook, eh!" Inspector Drew said to himself.

"And what motive does he have for wanting to murder you?"

Caspar made a face as though the whole subject was one distasteful to him.

"Largely fear," he said.

"Fear!"

"Yes, fear. He's a frightened man. He has good reason to be after cheating me out of a very large sum of money. I realise now how he engineered this whole thing." He looked across at the Inspector. "I'm not the sort of person who usually walks into traps, but I can see that that's just what I was due to do. My trouble was that I trusted Butcher. Even after he had cheated me, I was loth to reject him outright. I still believed we could come to some arrangement whereby he could work his passage back. The truth is," he added after a brief pause, "that Eddie Butcher has considerable charm and knows how to use it."

Drew thought that if he didn't step in quickly, his inquiry into Paula Caspar's death was in danger of drifting away on the tide of her husband's personal memoir of this man called Butcher.

"I must ask you to keep to the point," he said with greater firmness than he actually felt. "Have you any evidence that Butcher did come here this evening?"

"Only that that was the arrangement."

"Tell me about this arrangement please?"

"Butcher phoned me at my flat in town yesterday morning. He had been abroad for about two months and this was the first time we'd been in touch since he had gone off with this large sum of money belonging to me."

"How large?"

"Fifty thousand pounds."

Inspector Drew tried not to register the surprise which would immediately mark him as a country copper in Caspar's eyes; and then was cross with himself for caring what this wily crook might think of him. He gave a curt nod.

"Anyway Butcher phoned you?"

"Yes, and said he'd like to meet me."

"Up till then, you didn't know he was back in England?"

"No. His call came out of the blue. Took me completely by surprise."

"Did he say why he wanted to meet you?"

"No, he was very mysterious about it. Said he didn't want to discuss it on the telephone, that I was the first person he'd been in touch with since his return and that no one else knew he was back, and furthermore he didn't want anyone to know. However, he expressed this great anxiety to meet me."

"What was your reaction to that?"

"I agreed. One agrees to a good many things if one thinks there's a hope of retaining fifty thousand pounds. Even if it's only a faint hope, it's better than none at all. And that's where tonight's arrangement came in. As I say, Butcher insisted that the meeting should take place in conditions of the utmost secrecy and he asked if it wouldn't be possible for us to meet here. He knows this house and knows it's well secluded. So I agreed. It didn't matter to me where we met and I was pretty much in his hands since he wouldn't tell me where he was living—he was phoning from a public call box—and I had no means of getting in touch with him once he'd rung off. So you can see that he was in a strong position for dictating the terms of our meeting."

Inspector Drew had observed that Caspar had been fidgeting

with the fingers of his left hand all the time he'd been talking, as though he was trying to shake off bits of cobweb. This, however was the only sign of tension left. His earlier shocked appearance had gone. He now went on:

"The arrangement was that he should come here at half past ten and tap on the study window where I'd be waiting for him. I'd then let him in and after we'd finished, he'd leave again by the same way."

"Who suggested that?"

"He did. I'd told him I didn't know whether my wife would be at home or not and he asked if it would be all right to come to the french window, so that if she was in the house there'd be no question of her knowing of his visit."

"Does anyone else live here apart from you and your wife?"

"My sister-in-law, that is my wife's sister, acts as housekeeper, but she's abroad at the moment. Gone off to Spain on holiday."

Inspector Drew wanted to pinch himself to make sure he wasn't having one of the dreams that usually followed too many pickled onions with his bread and cheese supper: flats in London, lavish country homes, housekeepers who took holidays in Spain. This was the world of one of the most successful crooks in England. So successful that the police never came within touching distance of him. It was infinitely more dream-like than real. He mentally shook himself to break the hypnotised stare he'd been directing at the figure on the sofa in the beautifully cut, and perfectly worn, dark blue suit. The black leather slipers, the white shirt and sober blue tie. The head of iron grey hair, thick and curling at the neck.

"However, as I've already mentioned," Caspar went on, "I had to go up to town about seven o'clock and since I knew I wasn't going to be back by ten-thirty and had no way of getting in touch with Butcher to cancel our meeting. I told my wife of the arrangement and asked her to wait in the study and explain to him that I'd been called out." He paused. "I couldn't do anything else. I didn't want Butcher prowling around outside, and possibly scaring the wits out of my wife if she'd heard him and not known who it was. So I thought it best to tell her."

"Had it been arranged that the study window should be left unlocked?"

"No. I wasn't going to sit waiting for Butcher with it unlocked."

"But your wife seems to have?"

"She was very slightly deaf and may have unlatched it in

case she didn't hear his taps. I can't think of any other explanation."

"And you're suggesting that Butcher entered and shot your
wife as she sat in the chair with her back to the French
window?"

"I'm suggesting that he shot at the person sitting in the
chair believing it to be me. From behind you can only just see
the top of the head of anyone sitting in that chair and in the
sort of light there was in the room, you wouldn't be able to
distinguish the top of one head from another. You can test
that easily enough for yourself," he added condescendingly.
I'm suggesting that Butcher came intending to murder me,
only to discover that he'd murdered my wife instead." Grimly
he clenched one fist as though it held Butcher in its grasp.
"My poor, poor Paula!"

"Had your wife met Butcher before?" Drew asked, hurriedly.

"Yes, a few times."

"But they didn't know each other well?"

"No. She knew him as a business associate of mine. That's
all."

"You've told me that you agreed to meet Butcher as the
only hope of getting back the money he'd made off with?"

"Correct."

"Then what was it that cropped up which caused you to
cut the meeting? Why did you suddenly have to go up to
London at seven o'clock last night and leave your wife to
cope with this dangerous man? I can't think what can have
been more important to you than your meeting with Butcher.
But obviously something was! What?"

Inspector Drew's tone had grown in emphasis in the course
of this rolled-up piece of cross-examination, but even as he
concluded he knew that he had walked into the equivalent of
a granite cliff. Caspar's expression told him all too clearly not
to expect a squirm of discomfiture or any embarrassed evasion.
He had unsheathed his sword and it was just too bad that his
opponent was armed with the latest thing in revolvers.

"Certainly it was something important which caused me to
change my plans," Caspar said coldly. "Something even more
important than meeting Butcher."

"May I ask what it was?" Drew said with a somewhat half-
hearted lunge of his sword.

"An urgent business appointment." Caspar's finger was on
the trigger, but he was still delaying taking aim and firing, in-

evitable though Inspector Drew now felt that moment to be.

"May I ask with whom?" Another shadow lunge.

He knew it was coming now, smack between the eyes.

"With my solicitor, Mr. Haymore Jarvis, and my accountant, Mr. Bernard Pyxford," Caspar replied in a tone which made Inspector Drew wince. "When you're ready to write down what I've been telling you, I'll give you their addresses so that you can confirm with them that what I've told you is true."

"And this meeting was at your flat off Baker Street?" Drew asked, because he couldn't think of anything else to say.

"As I've already mentioned. It began around eight o'clock and finished at eleven, after which I drove down here." He gave Drew the sort of look a mamba might bestow on its selected victim. "I hope that disposes of your insinuation that I might have had anything to do with my wife's death." He touched the tip of his nose delicately, as if to make sure it was still there. "And now unless there is anything further you want to ask me, I'd like you to get my statement down in writing."

"Perhaps you would first give me a description of Butcher, so that I can circulate something on him straight away."

"I can do better," Caspar replied, feeling in his wallet pocket. "Here's a photograph of him."

As Inspector Drew took it, he wondered if Caspar carried around photographs of all his gang, perhaps even of Mr. Haymore Jarvis and Mr. Bernard Pyxford with their almost too-respectable sounding names.

An hour later the statement had been completed and signed, the body had been taken away to the local mortuary and Butcher's description was being spelt out on telex machines in police stations all over the country.

Detective-Sergeant Curtis came into the drawing-room where Inspector Drew was standing alone in apparent meditation.

"There are quite a few prints round that french window, sir. I imagine they have Caspar's in C.R.O. so we'll be able to eliminate his easily enough?"

Drew looked at him in a mildly thoughtful way before replying. "You might well imagine that C.R.O. would have the prints of the biggest crook in the country, but, in fact, I happen to know that they haven't."

"You mean, sir, that he's never been convicted of anything in the whole of his life," Sergeant Curtis asked incredulously,

"I mean just that. He's never even been acquitted. He's just never been tried."

"Then all we can do is to ask him to provide us with a nice set. I'm sure he'll be pleased to co-operate."

"It'll make me extremely suspicious if he *is*," Inspector Drew remarked glumly. "I've never been in such a crazy position before. It's as if one of our leading cat burglars had reported his own home broken into. It's positively embarrassing."

Sgt. Curtis grinned, "You think he probably murdered his wife himself then?"

"No, I don't think that. At least not yet. To be quite frank, I don't know what to think. And I shan't know what to think until we've found Butcher and been able to question him." He let out a short, breathy sigh, "I hope that we manage to lay our hands on him quickly."

11

Richard heard the news of Paula Caspar's death on the half past eight news that morning. He had woken up a few minutes previously and for several seconds his mind groped to discover why he felt as he did, sore-eyed and tacky and unrefreshed. Then like a lead weight settling on the bed of a pond, recollection returned. Four hours sleep and a new and baleful day waiting to be faced. He put out a hand to switch on the transistor radio and forced himself into wakefulness. The announcer's voice had the customary note of uncommitted brightness. Eager to be loved without any reciprocal involvement.

". . . The police have issued the description of a man who they believe may be able to help them in connection with their inquiries. He is Edmund Butcher, aged about thirty, and believed to be in the London area . . ."

He switched it off. So Eddie's fears had not been fanciful. Caspar had framed him.

Richard got out of bed and went into the kitchen to make himself a cup of coffee. He carried it into the bathroom and took gulps in between shaving. He wondered whether Eddie had heard the news bulletin. If he hadn't heard from him by the time he had dressed and had a second cup of coffee, he would phone him.

But Eddie had, in fact, heard it. His reaction was much the same as Richard's. In some ways it was a relief to have his fears confirmed. Reality, however grim, is never as testing on the nerves as anticipation. The fact that Caspar had closed the trap so briskly could even be seen as a hopeful sign. It showed that he had had it all planned, that it was contrived from start to finish. Nevertheless, he couldn't help wondering precisely what Caspar had told the police . . .

It was an hour later before Tony Tendo heard the news. His wife was still asleep and he kept the sound low so as not to disturb her. He had only turned the radio on for company and wasn't really concentrating when he caught Caspar's name.

"Hey, Bridge, wake up," he called, shaking her by the shoulder. "Listen to what they're saying on the news. It's about Ralph's wife. She's been murdered. Eddie Butcher did it." His voice was excited. "I'd better phone Jack. Looks like the end of our weekend. You heard what I been saying, Bridge?"

"Yes." Her tone was wide awake.

"That bastard Butcher! Fancy his killing poor old Paula!"

Bridget Tendo made no reply, but lay on her back staring thoughtfully at the ceiling. Her husband had, meanwhile, got through to the Ebonys, whose room was on the same floor.

"You just woken up, Jack? Then you haven't heard the news? Paula Caspar's been murdered and the police want to interview Eddie Butcher. The bastard must have had it all worked out, I reckon. If ever I get my hands on him, I'll squeeze him out of his skin. I guess one of us had better call Ralph straightaway . . . And, Jack, we'll have to arrange a wreath. A real nice one . . . What's that? . . . I know we don't know when the funeral is. But when we do, we'll have to send a wreath. That's all I'm saying . . . Look, Jack, you're not properly awake yet. But I think we ought to meet as soon as possible . . . Maybe there is nothing we can do, but Ralph needs us . . . Hey, wait a minute, Jack. Bridge is trying to say something . . . She suggests we wait for Ralph to get in touch with us. What do you think, Jack? . . . O.K. We'll wait then . . . Perhaps we could send a wreath from Brighton?" He rang off and shook his head slowly in bewilderment. "Poor old Ralph! Poor old Paula! What a bastard thing to do, killing old Paula!" He was lost in silent reflection for several seconds. "And what a bastard business having the police trampling around."

The reaction of Mr. Haymore Jarvis and Mr. Bernard Pyxford to the announcement of Paula Caspar's murder was identical. Each paused fractionally in what he was doing and then continued, in the case of Mr. Jarvis, with munching his breakfast cereal and, of Mr. Pyxford, with studying the racing page of the *Daily Express*.

Mr. Jarvis was a small, spare man with a bright, foxy expression and an alertness which had never been known to desert him during his waking hours. Like Richard Monk, he was the principal of a one-man firm. He had two managing clerks who were as well-known in every bar and betting shop within half a mile of the firm's offices in Marylebone High Street as they were in the courts of the district. Each deployed a measure of devious talent and charm which was exceeded only by that of Mr. Jarvis himself.

The great majority of the firm's clients were of the sort which the profession's governing body, the Law Society, prefers not to know about. In fact, it could be truthfully said that Mr. Jarvis prospered out of the British hypocrisy of pretending not to notice the bad smell in your neighbour's garden. Mr. Jarvis was quite ready to, and to offer his servieces—for a price.

He lived in a large, comfortable house at Mill Hill in North London and travelled to and from work in a chauffeur-driven Mark 10 Jaguar. He had no special hobbies, apart from indulging Mrs. Jarvis, with whom he was as much in love after thirty years as on the day he married her. Otherwise his work was everything to him. It was not a means to an end, but an end in itself.

Ralph Caspar had been his client for seven years and his most valuable one at that. It was in no small measure due to his solicitor that Caspar had not only kept the law at arm's length but had at the same time accumulated a large ill-gotten fortune.

Mr. Jarvis was having breakfast alone when he heard the news of his client's wife's death. His own wife always had her morning glass of hot water and slice of Ryvita up in their bedroom. He gave the radio a mildly interested glance as the announcer's voice went on its way to the next item, a tidal wave off the coast of Peru.

When their Spanish maid brought in his plate of bacon and eggs, she found him idly etching a pattern on the table cloth with his fork.

"Veree hot, Mr. Jarvis," she said as she put the plate in front of him.

"Thank you, Enrica," he said, as he contemplated the two pieces of crispy bacon and the brace of gleaming eggs. "And how are you this fine morning?" he inquired affably.

"Fine? It is not fine, Mr. Jarvis. It is nearly raining. There is no sun. It is not a fine morning."

"A façon de parler, Enrica," he explained benignly. "I just mean, how are you today?"

The girl looked at him like a dog trying desperately to fathom its master's mind.

"Today I have the slight gripe with my kidneys," she said

helpfully. "I put the sack with garlic next to them. It help, I think."

Mr. Jarvis nodded quickly and gazed at his bacon and eggs with slightly less relish than before he had initiated the conversation.

"I also eat the garlic," the girl went on remorselessly, "It is very good for the guts."

"So I've heard."

"Yes, it purges the poisons and, poof, . . ."

"I smell something burning in the kitchen," Mr. Jarvis said urgently, sniffing like a bloodhound on the trail.

It had the desired effect and Enrica made a rapid departure. Mr. Jarvis, applying mind over matter, set about enjoying the dish she'd put before him. He reckoned he could expect a call from Caspar within the next hour or so—and almost certainly one from the police as well. He viewed the police rather as an old Tom cat regards a bunch of roistering kittens. They might be a nuisance at times, but he always reckoned to have control of any situation in which he found himself involved with them. It had to be that way, if he was to keep clients like Ralph Caspar.

Mr. Bernard Pyxford felt much the same way. He was a short, plumpish man with a bald head and a pudgy bespectacled face. He could, at times, be almost intolerably jovial. In his own line of business, he was as able as Mr. Jarvis, but a penchant for the bottle and for backing anything which moved and was susceptible to receiving a bet made him a far more vulnerable person than the solicitor. It was the sort of vulnerability which Caspar found an exploitable asset in his associates. Indeed, where Mr. Jarvis could have managed without Caspar's business, Mr. Pyxford could not. His survival—that is, his next bottle of Scotch and his next wager— depended entirely on Caspar's continuing favour.

Mr. Pyxford's breakfast consisted of a glass of milk, well laced with whisky, which he drank standing in the bedroom of his bleakly furnished Notting Hill flat. Its therapeutic effect enabled him to move on to the next item of his daily agenda, which was to fetch the newsapaper from the front door and study the racing forecasts. This done, he would shave and get dressed and start working. He carried on business from the flat, so was saved the chore of travelling to and from an office. His wife had left him over ten years ago and he seldom thought of her any longer. For the time being, he was sufficiently aware of the realities of his situation to make himself give Caspar the service he expected and paid for.

On this particular morning, he turned on the radio in order to learn whether or not the afternoon's racing at Newton Abbot had been cancelled on account of the water-logged course. Instead, he heard of Paula Caspar's death.

He made a slight grimace and picked up the newspaper again. It was as if a small dark cloud had superimposed itself against his euphoric sky. The trouble was too many dark clouds blew these days—and always from the same direction.

Crumpling the paper under his arm, he went out to the kitchen in search of a second breakfast.

Beyond doubt the person most affected by the radio announcement of Paula Caspar's death was Diane Paisley. At least, it wasn't so much the fact of the murder, as of the police wish to get in touch with Eddie, that caused her to drop the cup of coffee she had in her hand at the time. She had gone into the small room at the back of the shop in which she and the other girl assistant had their morning coffee-break, and in which the transistor radio churned out the latest pops, at subdued volume, throughout the day for the benefit of Mrs. Oxley's ancient pekinese, which occupied a plump pale green satin cushion. When it wasn't dozing it exhibited all the signs of petulant old age.

Mrs. Oxley was the owner of the small dress-shop in the Lincolnshire market town which had been Diane's first stop after leaving London. Diane and Sally Hughes were her two assistants. The work scarcely justified two, but Mrs. Oxley had plans for opening a shop in a neighbouring town and her idea was that there would be a girl in charge of each while she shuttled between the two. She had been only too happy to acquire a girl with good London experience.

In answer to her customers' inquiries about Diane, she would say, "She's my new girl. Been working in the West end." Then lowering her voice to prevent Diane hearing, which she always did anyway, she would go on, "Left London after a break-up with her boy-friend. His loss, my gain. Nice girl, still a bit lovelorn, but getting over it . . . Now these new French chiffon scarves, Mrs. Brakespeare . . ."

"You all right?" Sally asked, sticking her head round the partition door and seeing the broken cup and the pool of milky coffee on the floor. "You look as though you've had a fright. Did Mr. Peng try and bite you?"

Mr. Peng had himself been disturbed by the noise and was glaring at both girls like an ageing bishop prematurely woken from his siesta.

Diane shook her head. "No, I'm all right. I just felt a bit queer." She stooped down and began to pick up the pieces of broken crockery.

"Here, you sit down. I'll see to that. I'll hear if anyone comes into the shop."

"Better not. You know Mrs. Oxley doesn't like us both away from the front at the same time. Honestly, I'm all right now. I'll clear this up and be with you in a few minutes."

"Sure?"

"Certain."

"You'd better make yourself another cup."

"No. I don't want any more. I'd drunk half of it."

Sally frowned. "You don't think it was something in the coffee made you feel ill? I thought it tasted a bit odd myself."

"No, I'm sure it was me and not the coffee."

At that moment, the shop door let out a warning ping and Sally scurried back to attend to a customer.

It took Diane no time at all to clean up the mess, though afterwards she had no recollection at all of the sequence of actions it had necessitated. Her mind swirled with one single thought. Eddie was back. Eddie was wanted for murder; for what else did that time-honoured euphemism about his being able to help the police with their inquiries mean but that he was their suspect?

When had he come back? And why? And how had he come to get caught up in Paula Caspar's murder? These and a dozen other questions swum about her head without the solace of any sort of answer. And worse, she had no means of getting in touch with him! It didn't occur to her to recollect that until she'd heard this thunderclap of news her rational self would have refused any suggestion that she would ever wish to see him again.

During the past two months, she had been making a slow recovery from the bruised and disoriented state in which the events surrounding her break with him had left her. Her heart and her conscience had both been deeply involved and finally, to no less an extent, her primitive instinct for survival.

She still remembered as a grim nightmare her being taken

86

to Caspar's flat and there having fear and terror put into her like an injection of some deadly serum.

There'd been no question of the courageous, tight-lipped heroine defying the villains in their lair. She'd told them all she knew of Eddie's plans, of Japan being his destination, of his transfer of funds to a Beirut bank. Happily—though it had seemed unhappily at the time—she'd known neither the name of the bank, nor that in which the money had been deposited.

And after they'd extracted from her every detail she could give them, Caspar had told her in a tone of quiet menace to get out of London that very day and never to return.

Looking back, that had been the most humiliating aspect of all. She had packed her bags and fled. Fled to Lincolnshire, a wealthy farming county to whose inhabitants London was either Sodom and Gomorrah rolled into one or the place where the nation's legislators wasted their time.

For the past two months she had been getting over the trauma of those final days in London, rationalising her actions and making by no means always successful attempts at self-justification.

The only thing which had emerged and become clear to her was that a chapter of her life was over, never to be re-opened. She had fallen in love with a young man who had everything save a sense of ethics. As a result she had been in danger of becoming caught up in the world of ugly violence and naked rapacity, but had escaped with a share of relatively minor lacerations. It was finished and over, and never again would she stand teetering on the edge of the criminal world. That had been her determination—until five minutes ago.

Now, Eddie, whom she'd gladly thought lost for ever on the other side of the world, was back and obviously in serious trouble, and her own particular world had again been thrown into sudden confusion.

"Are you sure you're all right, Diane?" Sally inquired, appearing in the doorway. "You still look like you'd seen a ghost. Why don't you go home and I'll explain to Mrs. Oxley."

Diane shook her head. "No, really I'm all right. I'm coming now."

But for the rest of the day, she never gave more than half her mind to what went on around her. The other half felt like an anaesthetised nerve as the drugged effect wears off.

12

While he was waiting for Eddie Butcher to come round to th
flat, Richard telephoned Alan Scarby and told him what ha
happened.

"In view of the police announcement, I'm proposing to rin;
the local station and tell whoever's in charge that Butcher ha
heard that they want to get in touch with him and that I'v
called to make an appointment."

"I take it you'll accompany him, Richard?"

"Certainly."

"What's your line going to be?"

"It depends on the questions they ask him."

"I appreciate that. But obviously at quite an early stage
you're going to have to advise Butcher how far he shoul
answer their questions. I mean, is he going to admit that h
went to Caspar's house last night or is he going to refuse t
answer that one?"

"My present feeling is that I ought to advise him to admi
everything he's told me. It takes the sting out when tha
happens."

"It's also a hellish risk," Alan remarked. "After all, the
mayn't have any proof that he was there, so why should But
cher forge one of the links in the chain of evidence agains
himself?"

"On the other hand, if he does decline, on my advice, t
answer that particular question and they *can* prove he wa
there by fingerprints or some such, it looks much worse. It'
the old story of the innocent man having nothing to hide."

"If you're lucky, you may get a clue as to how much th
police have found out."

"Hmm. Depends on how good they are at poker!" He paused
"But I reason in this way, Alan. Supposing Butcher tells th
police the whole story he told me. How he went to the house t
meet Caspar and instead found a dead body. The only evidenc
they can put against that will be Caspar's. Caspar will have t
be called to give his version of the arrangements ..."

"And you just don't see anyone accepting the word of an uncorroborated Caspar?"

"Precisely."

"It mayn't prevent their charging Butcher," Alan said doubtfully.

"But it'll prevent a jury convicting him."

"I think you're probably right, Richard, and that the best course would be for Butcher to be frank with the police. After all, if Casper *has* framed him, you can be pretty sure that he's left nothing to chance which he was able to fix in advance. He'll have seen to it that there is some handy piece of independent evidence which links Butcher with the crime. In which event, as you say, an admission by him that he did go to the house last night takes the sting out. There's nothing the police like better than a suspect denying something which they know they can prove anyhow."

"Denying doesn't really come into it, Alan. He either refuses to answer their questions or he tells them what he's told me."

"I know, but a refusal to answer questions in those circumstances will be equated with a denial by the police. And who'd blame them!" A sudden anguished shriek interrupted them. "Hang on a tick, Richard. I'm meant to be keeping an eye on Sophie and she's just gone like a meteor into the leg of the table." It was a couple of minutes before he returned. "Sorry about that. It's always happening. I think her radar malfunctions. Where were we? Oh, yes. I know what I was going to say. I assume you'll stay with Butcher the whole time, that is, until they charge him if they do?"

"I imagine so," Richard replied uncertainly.

"What I have in mind is that the police won't be exactly enthusiastic about your presence. On the other hand, if you insist upon staying until the interrogation is over, there can't be any question of Butcher remaining at the station for thirty-six hours or so allegedly *voluntarily,* as we should be assured later if the issue arose."

"No, I won't leave him to fester there alone. I think that's Butcher now, Alan. I heard a knock on the front door."

"Good luck. Let me know how things develop."

"Sure. Thanks for the help."

Eddie stepped quickly inside as soon as Richard opened the door.

"I feel as if every single person in London is looking for

me," he said bleakly.

"Come inside and relax."

"Relax! That's a hope when someone's snugly adjusting a noose round your neck."

"It's no less than expected," Richard reminded him.

Eddie, however, went on, "Quite frankly, I'd sooner have been sliced up in Japan than be framed for a murder on my return." Richard forebore to point out that this had certainly not been his attitude when they were actually in Japan. Then Eddie's sole thought was to survive until he reached home when, the inference had been, he'd be prepared to face all manner of skulduggery. "The thing I can't get over is Caspar using such tactics. I expected him to come at me armed with every weapon he could lay hands on, but not resort to fancy tricks like this. Getting the police to do his work for him just isn't his method." He shook his head in bewilderment. "To think I went down to that bloody house prepared for everything save a satin-lined trap. I was ready for him to open up from the roof with a cannon, but not for this, I was ready for any amount of firearms stuff, that's why..."

"That's why, what?"

"That's why I took a bit of hardware myself."

"Where is it now?"

"In the bottom of my suitcase."

"Unfired?"

"Certainly unfired."

Richard chewed, with a worried frown, at his lower lip. Eddie's gun could prove an embarrassment either way, retained or disposed of. However, so long as it couldn't be connected with the murder, he supposed its retention couldn't lead to trouble. Not grave trouble, that is. Though mere possession of it was an offence since he obviously didn't hold a firearms certificate for it. But that was a minor worry at this particular moment.

"Now listen to me," Richard said, "while I outline what I have in mind..."

For the next half hour they discussed the probable course of events after Eddie had presented himself at the police station. Then Richard went to the telephone and put through a call.

"I'd like to speak to Detective Inspector Drew, please. It's about the murder inquiry he's on. My name's Richard Monk. I'm a solicitor." Richard gave Eddie a smile as he waited to be put through to an extension. "Inspector Drew? Yes, that's right, Monk . . . Yes, a solicitor . . . I understand that you wish to interview Mr. Butcher in connection with the murder of Mrs. Caspar . . . He's a client of mine . . . Yes, I know exactly where he is. He's sitting in the room from which I'm making this call. I'm phoning you in order to make an appointment for Mr. Butcher and myself to see you." He placed a hand over the mouthpiece and said to Eddie with a sardonic grin, "If Caspar took you by surprise, it's nothing to what we've done to Inspector Drew and his boys." He removed his hand quickly. "Hello . . . yes . . . That'll suit Mr. Butcher and myself. We should reach you in about an hour . . . What's that? . . . I'm speaking from my home . . . Berkeley 4306 . . . My office is in Bedford Square, you'll find me in the *Law List* . . ."

After he'd rung off, he remarked to Eddie, "You might have thought I was trying to buy the police station with a dud cheque. We may even find the door bolted against us when we arrive."

It took them just under an hour to reach the sub-station where Detective Inspector Drew had set up his headquarters. It was one which had been opened only a year before and gave the impression that the architect had lost interest before the roof was put on. Its utility appearance was emphasised by the company it kept, surrounded as it was by the homes of the rich.

It would be untrue to say that policemen literally surrounded the car as Richard drew up in front of the station. On the other hand, two materialised on either side before he had time to switch off the engine.

"Drive round to the yard at the back, sir," said one, who was in fact Detective-Sergeant Curtis. "That way you'll avoid the press."

Richard did as he was bidden and then, with Eddie close at his side, followed Sergeant Curtis into the station.

"Watch out along this passage, sir," Curtis said cheerfully over his shoulder, "although it's a new building, the floor's begun to disintegrate. Also mind your hand on the banister as we go upstairs, the wood's splintered in several places. Marvellous, isn't it!"

He threw open a door marked C.I.D. and stood aside for them to enter.

Inspector Drew, who had watched their arrival in the yard from the window, came round the edge of the desk. He had been giving anxious thought to the requirements of protocol at such a meeting. In the event, he contrived to shake hands with Richard, but not with Eddie without this appearing too obvious.

"I suggest that the best thing will be for you to ask what questions you want, Mr. Drew," Richard said, "and I'll advise my client whether or not he should answer them. Will that be convenient?"

As Richard well knew, there could scarcely have been anything less convenient to the inspector, who would obviously have liked to have had Eddie alone to question, to cajole, to threaten, to seduce with station tea and cigarettes, to lock up in a cell and then produce at will for further questioning. And all in the good name of voluntarily assisting the police. That's what Inspector Drew or any other normal-minded officer would have liked! The more so, as he'd been up all night and was feeling every one of his forty-two years, with a fifteen per cent bonus into the bargain.

"I hope, Mr. Monk," Inspector Drew said with a mildly pained expression, "that you will remember I'm investigating a case of murder and that you won't encourage your client to adopt an obstructive attitude to my questioning."

"I'm sure we both know exactly where we stand," Richard replied blandly, uncapping his pen and turning back the cover of the foolscap pad which was balanced on his knee.

Inspector Drew winced. He'd sooner have had the Chief Constable breathing down his neck than Richard sitting there like a recording angel. His opening questions were in the nature of ranging shots and Eddie answered each of them, after a quick nod from Richard.

Yes, he'd known Mr. Caspar for several years; yes, he'd met Mrs. Caspar once or twice; yes, he had been to "Woodlands."

"Did you go there last night?" Drew asked, cocking his head on one side.

Richard and Eddie had agreed beforehand that he should answer this question if it came in a direct form.

"Yes, I did."

Richard realised at once from the Inspector's expression that they'd made the right decision. Far from looking pleased at this useful admission, he appeared positively crestfallen. That could only mean that they had independent proof of Eddie's presence at the house.

"What time did you go there?" he asked in a flat tone.

"About half-past ten."

"What did you find?"

Eddie glanced once more at Richard, who gave him a nod. He then related to the Inspector the story, almost word for word, as he had told it to Richard in the small hours of that same morning.

When he finished, Inspector Drew gazed at him like a man who finds that his money has dropped through a hole in his pocket and that he'll have to walk five miles home.

"You're as good as saying that Mr. Caspar has framed you!" he finally exclaimed in an affronted tone.

"That shouldn't afford you much surprise if you know anything about Mr. Caspar," Richard said bluntly. "I should have expected the police to be fairly wary about accepting his word."

"That's your opinion, sir," Inspector Drew said in a defensive tone.

"Anyway," Eddie broke in, "not even Caspar can pin a motive on me for murdering his wife. I've told you I scarcely knew her. Why should I want to kill her? Has he told you that?"

"He has suggested that you intended to murder him. That you fired through the back of the chair, thinking it was he who was sitting in it."

"But that's absolutely crazy!"

"Our scientific experts will tell us whether or not it's crazy," Inspector Drew said stiffly. "Do you admit that you had a motive for murdering Mr. Caspar?"

"You suggest one," Eddie replied, but not too confidently.

"You'd recently absconded with a large sum of money belonging to Mr. Caspar."

"He told you that?"

"Is it true?"

Richard leaned across and whispered in Eddie's ear.

"I don't wish to answer that question," Eddie said in a faintly sulky tone.

Richard had intervened since he didn't wish Eddie to become entangled by questions about his flight from England before they knew exactly what gloss Caspar had placed on those events. It seemed unlikely that Caspar had said anything which would provide the police with an opportunity of, so to speak, looking at his books. That would be the last thing he would want and he could scarcely throw any mud at Eddie without a fairly large clod of the stuff being hurled back at him. No, Richard couldn't believe Caspar had said anything which might expose his own whole elaborate edifice of fraudulent business. Expose and undermine.

It was at this point that Inspector Drew cautioned Eddie and asked him if he wished to make a statement in writing.

There was another short, whispered consultation and then Richard said, "My client welcomes the opportunity of signing a written record of all that he has told you. As has already been made clear, he has nothing to hide."

Inspector Drew let out a perceptible sigh. He knew he shouldn't have sighed, but the fact was that he felt the interview had increased his problems rather than solved any of them. "I'm afraid it'll take some time to write everything down. Detective-Sergeant Curtis here is the pen-pusher. Just before we start, there is one other matter. Have you any objection to my taking possession of the clothes you were wearing last night?"

Eddie glanced at Richard who shook his head.

"Where are they?"

"They're what I've got on."

"Then, perhaps while your statement is being recorded, an officer could go and fetch you some spares."

Eddie glanced at Richard in consternation. In the first place it meant disclosing that he had been living under a false name, and that was liable to all manner of misinterpretations by the police. In the second, they'd be sure to find his gun. Let them inside his bedroom and they'd be through everything like driver ants.

"What's the address?"

Richard thought fast. Even if he suggested going himself, Drew would politely insist upon an officer accompanying him, and any demurrer would only increase police suspicions. Also, it was inevitable that the police would find out about the false name under which he had registered. Better once more to admit and remove the sting.

He said, "Mr. Butcher has been staying at the Greenway Hotel near Gloucester Road. He's registered there under the name of Roy Smith. He did this purely for reasons of personal safety."

"Is that so?" Drew inquired with a spurt of interest. Eddie nodded. "What were you afraid of?"

"Caspar."

A shutter fell across Inspector Drew's expression. He might

have guessed. Allegation and counter-allegation by a couple of trained villains, and he caught in the middle.

"Are the clothes you need out, or in a suitcase?" Richard asked.

"They're all in my suitcase."

"Then all you have to do is fetch that," Richard remarked, turning to Inspector Drew.

It required no clairvoyant to see what was passing through the mind of each at this moment. Drew and Curtis fell to contemplating the possibilities of quietly searching it, while Richard and Eddie were wondering how this could be frustrated. The fact that it was locked meant nothing. If the police didn't have a key which fitted, then it would be subjected to a handy accident which would cause it to burst open and scatter its contents.

Richard felt that he could only utter a veiled warning and leave it at that.

"You are, of course, entering Mr. Butcher's hotel room with his permission and without any legal right. I hope that permission won't be abused."

"Abused, Mr. Monk?" Inspector Drew managed to sound genuinely surprised.

"Yes, namely that your officer merely enters the room, picks up the suitcase and brings it here to Mr. Butcher."

"Oh, I see what you mean." A slow smile spread across Inspector Drew's face, but he said nothing further.

The completion of Eddie's statement and the arrival of his suitcase coincided within a few minutes. The young detective-constable, who had been sent to fetch it, brought it into Inspector Drew's office and placed it with almost elaborate care over on a chair.

"You have the key?" Drew inquired politely. Seeing Eddie's frown, he went on, "Surely you have no objection to opening it in my presence?"

Eddie looked at Richard who said stonily, "No, go ahead."

The whole thing had been so smoothly managed that they were standing on board before they realised that the carpet had been pulled from under their feet.

After the case had been opened and Eddie had extracted a spare set of clothes, Inspector Drew who had been watching intently stepped forward.

"You don't mind my having a look?"

"Is it any use minding?" Richard asked frostily.

"Probably not, but I always feel that it's the minor courtesies which help to keep our relations with the public nicely oiled." Inspector Drew's tone was a purr. It was clear he had sensed that a triumph lay not far out of sight.

When his hands, groping like those of a diligent Customs Officer, came to the gun, he stood suddenly stock-still. Then he extracted it with infinite care as though he might have been defusing a highly sensitive bomb. He laid the weapon delicately on a clean sheet of paper on his desk.

"Yours?"

"Yes, but you'll find it hasn't been used for . . ."

"For how long?"

"Not since I returned to England five days ago."

"You brought it into the country with you?"

"My client didn't say that," Richard intervened. "Further‑ more, I shall advise him not to answer that question."

Inspector Drew shrugged. "Take Mr. Butcher somewhere to change his clothes. I want those he has got on, and this gun, to be taken to the lab as soon as possible." After they'd left the room and only Richard himself remained, he said, "Would you like a cup of tea or coffee, while we're waiting, Mr. Monk?"

"I could certainly do with a cup of coffee."

"It won't be the real thing."

"That's all right. I actually prefer instant coffee."

"Good lord!" Inspector Drew sounded shocked.

After a pause, Richard said, "Off the record, Mr. Drew, I'll tell you that Butcher's version of events which he's just given you is precisely the same as he gave me."

"I must say he didn't lose much time in finding himself a lawyer."

"As a matter of fact, he'd secured my services—or at least my interest—when we happened to meet in Japan . . ."

Richard reckoned that there was nothing to be lost in giving Drew the general background. Namely that Caspar and But‑ cher had had a disagreement and Butcher had fled, but had returned because he couldn't settle down abroad. He made no further mention of the alleged defalcation, nor did he refer to Diane Paisley by name.

When he had finished his recital, he paused and said, "I don't imagine I have to tell you what an arch-villain Caspar is. From all I've heard he's the nearest thing to a criminal tycoon we've ever had in this country."

"I'm not disputing that, Mr. Monk. Equally there can't be any dispute that someone murdered his wife, and I have to investigate murders with equal energy whether the victims are innocent babes or hardened thugs. The law doesn't distinguish between them. The only thing is that cases involving the likes of Mr. Caspar are that much tougher going. You're apt to feel you're being used and not co-operated with."

"May I ask whether Caspar has an alibi for the murder?"

"He was attending a sudden and urgent business meeting in London. Two professional gentlemen he was with at the time have confirmed that this was so."

Richard nodded grimly. "Of course, if he is framing my client, one would expect him to have an alibi."

"If it's any help to you, Mr. Monk, I wouldn't trust Mr. Caspar with a penny stamp. I'd want corroboration if he told me my name was Archibald Drew. But that doesn't mean that he's incapable of telling the truth or that he can never be believed about anything. All it does mean is that my job is made much more difficult, in addition to the distaste of suddenly finding myself in the same camp as an out-an-out villain." He shrugged. "But life is full of ironies—especially a policeman's." Giving Richard a rueful smile, he added, "One thing I don't mind telling you within these four grubby walls, I'd have given anything for it to have been Caspar who was murdered rather than his wife. Rather than anyone."

"I'm sure you would have," Richard remarked drily. "Incidentally, I take it that once my client has handed over his clothing he's free to leave?"

Inspector Drew expelled a gust of breath and appeared to be troubled by grave uncertainty. "If you'll excuse me, I must go and make a phone call," he said abruptly and left the room.

While he was gone, Richard tried to decide whether or not he would charge Eddie Butcher with murder if he was in the inspector's position. Nobody could say that there was no evidence. On the other hand, it was shot through with unresolved doubts. It must all depend on how far they felt able to rely on Caspar. And surely that couldn't be very far! British justice really was seen through a looking-glass when Ralph Caspar was put forward as chief witness for the Crown.

It was nearly fifteen minutes before Inspector Drew returned. In an expressionless voice, he said, "Will you come downstairs, Mr. Monk? Butcher is just about to be charged with the murder of Mrs. Caspar."

13

Tendo and Ebony had cut short their weekend at Brighton and had come hurrying back to London to be at the side of their boss. Their wives had, however, elected to stay on and await events.

The two men had returned in Tendo's new Jaguar and gone straight to Caspar's flat. There they found him looking drawn and haggard as neither could ever recall having seen him before. He was also sunk in a morose silence from which he showed no inclinaton to emerge.

"Paula's death has really smacked him," Tendo observed to his companion, when Caspar had left the room for a few minutes.

Ebony nodded.

"Poor old Paula!" Tendo murmured, as he had done regularly since first hearing the news. "I know how I'd feel if someone killed my Bridge. What's more I'd settle that score without any assistance from the police!"

Ebony still said nothing. He frequently didn't when Tendo rambled on in this way. Although they were Caspar's two senior hatchet men and were as much a team as Laurel and Hardy, they were utterly dissimilar in most ways. For one thing, Jack Ebony was the more intelligent, and though he appreciated Tony Tendo's muscular brawn, he had scant respect for his brainpower.

Caspar came back into the room.

"I'd like you to go down to the police station, Jack, and try and find out what's happening," he said. "Pretend you're a press-man or something. See if they've got on to Butcher yet."

"Sure," Ebony gave an understanding nod. "I'll take your car, Tony. O.K.?"

"O.K. But mind how you drive, boy, I don't want it thumped."

Ebony smiled thinly. In fact, each of them was a first-class driver who could have sailed through the advanced test if he hadn't scorned to take it.

Left alone with Caspar, Tendo fingered the black crêpe armband he had dashed out and bought before leaving Brighton. He was also wearing a narrow black tie, shiny as a strip of liquorice.

"Why do you think he did it, Ralph?" he asked. "Was it simply to spite you?"

"No. I don't think he meant to kill Paula. He meant to shoot me. He thought it was me sitting in the chair."

"The dirty bastard," Tendo muttered with feeling. "And all while you were in the flat here with Haymie and Bernie."

If there was one thing which Mr. Haymore Jarvis objected to more than anything else, it was being called Haymie by Tony Tendo. But happily he wasn't present to register his annoyance on this occasion. Mr. Pyxford, on the other hand, had no reservations; For all he cared, anyone could call him anything.

Caspar nodded. "Yes. I heard from Fukiko in Tokyo yester-. day about the movement of some gold bullion out of Hong Kong. There was a chance of moving in on the deal, if a quick decision was made. But it was going to be a costly business and I had to find out how we were likely to come out of it. Pyxford advised against in the end. I had Jarvis along as there was some nonsense about forged bills of lading. Anyway, we decided nothing doing. There were too many risks for too small a profit. Trouble was that Fukiko hadn't got on to it in time."

"That Fukiko's a pretty smart boy usually," Tendo remarked.

"I'm beginning to wonder. He bungled Eddie Butcher's removal and now this."

"But he's better than Shima."

"Shima lacked moral fibre," Caspar said grimly. "He cracked under fire. Men like that are no good to me."

"Men like Butcher," Tendo added, nodding. "He didn't have any moral fibre either."

Caspar frowned. Tendo could display a remarkable degree of wooden stupidity at times. Whatever was wrong with Eddie Butcher, it'd had nothing to do with his moral fibre. At least, not within Caspar's context. If anything, he'd had too much moral fibre. He hadn't been sufficiently afraid not to abscond. No, when Ralph Caspar spoke of moral fibre, he did so in terms of security risks. Anyone who was liable to open his mouth too wide if he happened to fall into the police net was a poor risk. And there were only two ways of dealing with that. But the police! I mean once you invite the police into your backyard . . ."

"Use your headpiece, Tony. Anyway, what's so frightening about the police! Provided you keep them in their place," he added, his expression becoming grimly serious all of a sudden. He put up a hand to shield his eyes and was silent for half a minute.

"Let me get you a drink," Tendo said.

Caspar removed his hand and shook his head slowly, his eyes revealing a look of apprehension that Tendo had never seen there before, but which he could understand in the circumstances. He must, for all his pretence, be worried about the intervention of the police in his affairs. There came into Tendo's mind a proverb he'd once been told by a silvery-tongued Arab. It was: never take a camel into your tent. He had remembered it because it had made him laugh. Well, inviting the assistance of the police when you lived outside the law was like taking a camel into your tent.

The silence which had fallen between them was relieved by the telephone ringing. Caspar answered it and immediately recognised Ebony's voice at the other end of the line.

"They've got Butcher and he's been charged with Paula's murder," he said in an exultant tone.

Caspar gave a low nod of satisfaction. "Where did they pick him up?"

"I gather he gave himself up." A frown formed on Caspar's face and grew when Ebony added, "Complete with lawyer. A solicitor called Richard Monk. I saw him drive away alone about ten minutes ago."

"Monk," Caspar repeated, as though savouring the full flavour of Richard's name. "Find out what you can about him before you come back. Did you learn anything else?"

"I was talking to one of the crime reporters hanging round the place and he thought the police had been rather pushed into charging him."

"In what way?" Caspar's tone was icily suspicious.

"He gathered that the presence of the solicitor pressured them into a decision. They either had to charge him or let him go. If he hadn't been accompanied by his lawyer, they could have kept him at the station much longer while making up their minds. The old war of nerves stuff."

"Have you found out what Eddie has said to the police?" Caspar asked sharply.

" 'Fraid not. The police are not saying anything beyond the fact that he's been charged. Nothing's leaked out at all. He'll be coming up in the local Magistrates' Court on Monday morning, they say."

"I'll get Jarvis to attend," Caspar said. "I'll phone him right away."

He rang off, leaving Ebony still holding the receiver to his ear.

14

Detective-Inspector Drew knew very well that this was not a case in which he would be quietly left to assemble all the pieces without external distractions. In the first place, it immediately attracted enormous public interest, with the newspapers vying with one another in ingenuity in not over-stepping the bounds which might lay them open to contempt of court proceedings. Their single objective was to nudge their combined readership into recalling all that it had ever heard of Ralph Caspar, without explicitly repeating details which were (a) contempt of court and (b) libellous. Thus the public were reminded that the dead woman's husband was the well-known business man, reputed millionaire said some, whose name had been associated with cut-price car insurance and various other activities of equally dubious standing. What they all longed to print, of course, were columns of intriguing speculation on what lay behind the death of a high-class English gangster's wife. If only it could have been used, it was the most wonderful hook on which to hang such stories as would have warranted doubling the price of their various papers. In the event, however, they cursed, swore and sighed, and sailed as close to the wind as they dared.

But the public wasn't alone in exhibiting interest. Inspector Drew's colleagues in other forces, especially those in the Met, showed a heavy concentration of professional interest in what had happened. One result of this was that within a few hours of Butcher's being charged, a high-powered conference was held which was presided over by the Detective Chief Superintendent of the C.I.D. and attended by officers from the Yard Fraud and Flying Squads and the Home Counties Regional Crime Squad.

They were all men to whom Caspar represented a live, undercover inquiry of some sort. One had been burrowing for months into the activities of one of his companies and had been reduced to feeling like a lost speleologist. Another had been investigating his possible link with a racket concerning the illicit diversion of materials from large construction sites. Yet another with his reputed behind-the-scenes connection with a recent rash of commercial diamond thefts.

All of them, Inspector Drew was satisfied to observe, were as non-plussed by the turn of events as he himself had been.

"I never thought we'd come to this," one senior officer said gloomily. "Ralph Caspar's evidence the main plank in the Crown's case on a criminal charge. I know what I'd do if I was on the jury."

The Detective Chief Superintendent tut-tutted. "The man's wife has been murdered and there's a good case against Butcher. Since when have the police been able to choose their witnesses? If the jury don't believe Caspar's evidence, they don't, but that doesn't mean we can ignore it. You're as good as saying that because he's a crook, he isn't entitled to the same protection of the law as an honest man."

The logic of this was irrefutable and they all knew it. It was a Flying Squad officer who asked, "Can the possibility of his having killed her himself be completely excluded?"

"His solicitor and accountant confirm that they were having a business conference with him in London at the time the murder was committed," Inspector Drew replied.

"I wonder! I agree you can't do much in the face of that, but personally I regard those two as trickier than their client, just because they do wear the respectable garb of their professions. Believe me, they're both bent. They're so bent they'd make a corkscrew straight."

"The point is," the Detective Chief Superintendent said a trifle impatiently, "there's no evidence that Caspar had a motive for murdering his wife. Unless you're suggesting he sacrificed her simply in order to frame Butcher. And I don't know how on earth you could ever hope to prove that even if it were true."

"I wouldn't put it past him," the same officer replied. "But more to the point, I did hear a rumour a couple of months back that he was after some other woman. My informant only had it third hand himself and no names were mentioned. Moreover, Ralph Caspar has always been extremely discreet in the handling of his private life."

"He's been a darned sight too discreet in the handling of his business life as well," someone grumbled. "The trouble now is that he operates behind so many protective screens we never get within sniffing distance of him."

Inspector Drew said, "Certainly our information down here bears out that he and his wife largely went their own ways, but they still lived together and there's never been any suggestion of scandal."

"That's a good word to use in connection with Caspar," someone said scornfully. "Isn't his whole existence a national scandal?"

And so the conference pursued its course to a desultory end. Everyone agreed to keep their ears more sharply open than usual and to maintain close touch with Inspector Drew, to whom they wished good luck without any sign of confidence that it would come his way.

The Detective Chief Superintendent had the final word.

"I think the best we can all hope for is that when the case is over, Butcher may feel inclined to offer us a bit of co-opera-tion. If that happens, we may be able to begin to slide the skids under Master Caspar. But until that moment arrives, everyone would be well advised to remember that he's a Crown witness and should be treated with as much caution as if he were radioactive."

15

Richard had driven back to London, depressed and worried, after leaving Eddie Butcher at the police station.

He felt he was responsible for his client having been charged; that he had not given him the right advice. In a word, that he had loused things up.

He was still awash with self-reproach when he arrived at his flat. He immediately phoned Alan.

"I can't help feeling it would have been better if I'd advised him not to answer their questions. As it is, we've gratuitously corroborated Caspar's evidence about the arrangements for the visit and the prosecution will be able to say in effect, 'you see Caspar *can* be believed. He *is* telling the truth. He mayn't be the nicest sort of person, but that doesn't mean he can tell only lies.' In fact, what Butcher has done, as a result of my advice, is establish Caspar's credibility. It's too late, now, Alan, but I ballsed it—and ballsed it badly."

"I don't think you have. At least not necessarily so. After all, supposing he hadn't chosen to admit his presence at Caspar's house and the prosecution can produce irrefutable proof that he was there. Things immediately look much blacker for him than they need. The jury, with their simple logic, would say to themselves: an innocent man wouldn't have been afraid to have told the police he was there. But this man didn't and yet we know he *was* there. The only inference is that he isn't an innocent man. Q.E.D." He paused, "Quite frankly, Richard, it's too early to tell whether you gave him the right advice or not. So it's certainly too soon to start agonising about it. Anyway, it's unlike you to fuss and bite your nails."

Richard gave a short, rueful laugh. "I'm rather more involved in this case than I've ever been before."

"It'll teach you not to pick up clients when you go off holidaying on the other side of the world," Alan said heartlessly. "Also, have you thought of this? Perhaps Butcher did murder Mrs. Caspar."

"No! I'm certain he didn't. I'm sure I'd have . . ."

"You'd have what?"

"Known it in my water if he had."

"Forget your water and shake off the spell Butcher seems to have cast over you. He could have done it just as Caspar has suggested. Could have!"

"Could have, but didn't," Richard said obstinately.

"For God's sake, Richard! Just because Caspar is a Goliath in crime doesn't make Butcher a David. On his own admission, he's an amoral, swindling crook. The fact that he's swindled a bigger crook, doesn't alter the basic facts."

"Are you saying that you don't want to be associated with the case?" Richard asked stiffly.

"What's got into you!" Alan exclaimed. "Of course I want to be associated with it, if you're willing to brief me."

"I imagined from what you've been saying that you'd sooner not have a swindling crook for a client." His tone was still stiff.

There was a pause and then Alan chuckled. "He won't be the first or last I've had in that category. It's just that some are more engaging than others. Clearly Butcher stands high in the charm stakes."

"I'm sorry Alan, I didn't mean to get so huffy. But I am worried about the chap. And for all you say, I do still reproach myself."

"I'm equally sure you don't need to." With a change of tone he went on, "I'd suggest your coming along and having a drink this evening, but Jane and I are going to a cocktail party down the road. So what can I suggest you do to take your mind off holding post mortems with yourself? What about a run round Hyde Park?"

"I might even do that, Except that it'll be *in* rather than round."

"Followed by a hot bath, a drink and an early night."

"Could be," Richard replied non-committally, it having come to him with sudden force that he would like to spend the evening with Sarah.

He rang her as soon as he had finished talking to Alan and felt a tingle of delight when she said that she would sooner come round than go to a concert at the Festival Hall with someone called Roger, who had only asked her at the last minute and then told her to find her own way and arrive fed, as he himself was going out to a bachelor dinner party afterwards.

She arrived at the flat just as Richard was about to set off on his run. She examined him with an amused smile as he stood in the hall in his blue windcheater and flimsy white shorts.

"It's the night of the Mayfair Olympics," he said.

"Oh, is that it! I thought you'd put it on especially for me."

"I'll take it all off specially for you."

"I think you'd better go and have your run," she said, propelling him gently toward the door.

When he returned half an hour later, he found her in the kitchen. She was singing to herself and had enough pots on the stove to give promise of a five-course dinner.

"I hope you don't mind me presuming to cook our dinner."

"Delighted."

"I rather enjoy cooking."

"So do I."

"Really?"

"Really."

"You don't just mean sausages and steaks under the grill?"

"No, I mean real cooking, I have six specialities of the house I can do."

"Tell me one?"

"Real Hungarian Goulash."

"And another?"

"Fillet of sole Walewska."

"I believe you."

"For that, I'll fetch you a drink."

Later, much later, he said, "Do you need to go home tonight?"

She didn't answer immediately, then said, "I don't need to, but I think I should—at any rate tonight."

16

It was raining on Monday morning and the traffic along the King's Road and through Fulham was worse than ever. Even though Richard was driving against the incoming stream, it was still awful and he began muttering threats of violence when he got stuck behind a ballast lorry which was throwing off a fine spray of watery sand, as well as snorting out a plume of thick diesel fumes. At the top of Putney High Street, he at last managed to overtake it and did so with his engine screaming its own sense of frustration.

As he forked left along the Kingston by-pass, he realised that he would arrive at court only just in time and probably have no opportunity of speaking to Eddie before the formal hearing began.

He was still inwardly fretting over the advice he had given him, added to which Alan had successfully stirred a small worm of doubt in his mind about Eddie Butcher. Alan had expressed an objective view, uncoloured by any personal acquaintance with him. Richard had rejected it. But ever since he had been wondering.

Had Eddie fooled him one hundred per cent? Was he still up to his neck in villainy? Was the whole Japanese episode an exercise in soft-soaping? And, most important of all, had he all the time been deftly preparing for what had now happened, namely his being charged with murder?

Richard remembered how he had seized every opportunity of emphasising how his life was in danger from Caspar; how Caspar wouldn't think twice about exterminating him; how he could only muster the courage to return to England if Richard would agree to represent him in whatever befell. Well, something had befallen him all right. It was almost as though he had predicted it, when he looked back.

Alan had a good point when he said one shouldn't pick up clients on holiday. Not that he had picked one up, Richard reflected ruefully. On the contrary, the client had picked him up. Deliberately and, to use one of the law's chosen phrases, with malice aforethought.

It was a couple of minutes before half-past ten when he thrust his way into the small court-house. A policeman on the court-room door stuck out a firm arm barring his entrance.

"Yes, sir?" he inquired, eyeing Richard coolly.

"My name's Monk. I'm Butcher's solicitor."

"In that case you'd better go in, sir," he said gravely, opening the door with one hand and using the other to bar the way of two women who were trying to slip past at the same time.

The court-room was packed and Richard still had to fight his way through to the lawyers' seats at the front. All the national papers, as well as the B.B.C. and I.T.N. had sent down reporters for the occasion. So much for Caspar's drawing power, Richard reflected. The local reporters clearly regarded the invasion with the same distaste and annoyance as the customers of the village shop who find it suddenly besieged by bargain-hunters from a neighbouring town.

Richard squeezed into a seat and pulled a notebook out of his briefcase. The magistrates hadn't yet taken their places and the atmosphere was that of a first-night audience before the curtain goes up.

"Good morning. Are you Mr. Monk?"

Richard turned to his neighbour who had addressed him and who was now gazing at him with quizzical interest. He was a small man with sharp, alert eyes. But Richard's first impressions were of rings on fingers and a strong smell of lavender water. In fact, he wore two rings on one hand and one on the other, but they were the sort of rings which drew attention to themselves.

"My name's Haymore Jarvis. I'm here on Mr. Caspar's behalf. Just a watching brief." He held out the more heavily-ringed hand. "I don't think we've met before."

"No, I don't believe we have," Richard replied. So this was Mr. Haymore Jarvis! The old saying about velvet gloves over mailed fists might have been coined for him. Here, at a glance, was high-powered smoothness and steely competence rolled into one.

"Will you be taking the case yourself through the Magistrates' Court or instructing Counsel?"

"I haven't decided yet," Richard said.

"Similarly, I suppose it's too early to have decided on your line of defence?"

Richard nodded and ostentatiously opened his notebook and

began writing in it. Mr. Haymore Jarvis was the last person he'd confide any defence secrets in. Hell, their professional interests couldn't be further apart!

"Have you known your client a long time?" Mr. Jarvis now asked in an apparently casual tone.

"Not particularly," Richard said, without looking up. He would, however, have been less than happy if he'd been aware that Caspar's solicitor knew exactly where and when he'd first met Eddie Butcher.

"He used to work for my client at one time," Mr. Jarvis went on.

"So I gather."

"They had a bust-up a few months ago. I expect you heard that, too? My client, however, never believed he'd really carry out his threats."

"Threats?"

"To get even with Mr. Caspar for some imagined wrong."

"Oh, I see!"

Mr. Jarvis waited for Richard's further response and when none came, he turned his attention to the newspaper which lay folded in front of him.

After a time Richard lent back and subjected his neighbour to a covert examination. Mr. Jarvis certainly dressed the part. He was wearing a black jacket and waistcoat and striped trousers. A fat pearl on the end of a gold pin nestled just below the knot in his tie. Far from being out of place, the rings and the aroma of lavender water were clearly as much a part of him as the scent and the petals are part of a rose. He put Richard in mind of someone who had gone to an old-fashioned firm of outfitters and asked to be decked out in correct legal garb. By contrast Richard felt positively raffish in his dark grey flannel suit and wide-striped Turnbull and Asser shirt with button-down collar and black knitted silk tie.

Mr. Jarvis pushed the newspaper from him and glanced at the gold watch on his wrist. It was one of those dust-proof, water-proof, shock-proof ones the size of a small scone that is guaranteed to show the correct time at the bottom of the ocean in addition to other unlikely places in which watch-wearers may find themselves.

"They're late," he remarked, throwing Richard a sidelong look. "Are they always in this court?"

"I've no idea. I've not been here before."

"Any idea of the date they're going to fix for the hearing?"

Richard shook his head. "I hope it'll be as soon as possible."

"You do?"

"Certainly. My client doesn't want to be kept hanging around waiting for his trial."

"You make it sound as if you're confident of the outcome," Mr. Jarvis observed with a quickening of interest. "And even before you've heard the prosecution's evidence!"

Richard met his searching gaze with an impassive expression. So long as Caspar's solicitor continued to fish, let him be uncertain what he'd caught.

"Are you likely to do much cross-examination in the lower court?" he asked, casting his line again.

"That depends on what the witnesses say in evidence. I suppose you're really wondering about your own client? Whether I'll cross-examine him?"

"It would certainly help my—and his—arrangements to know."

I bet it would, too, Richard thought. "I'm afraid I can't help you over that," he said. "It obviously depends on circumstances." With a slight bite to his tone, he added, "Anyway, I'm sure Mr. Caspar will understand that his personal convenience is a small matter compared with serving the cause of justice."

Mr. Jarvis's expression hardened and he gave Richard a look of genuine unfriendliness. That was fine by Richard in his present mood. Let the other side realise that this would be a no-holds-barred fight and be left wondering what the defence had in their armoury.

If Eddie was telling the truth and if Caspar had neatly framed him, then almost certainly Mr. Jarvis was, himself, in on the crookery. Richard returned his look of cold dislike.

It was at this, perhaps fortunate, moment that the magistrates entered and took their places on the bench. The clerk, who had a self-important air, sat down at the desk immediately below the dais and affected to ignore everyone within sight. When he was satisfied that all eyes were on him, he said in a peremptory tone, "Put up Edmund Stephen Butcher."

Eddie came through a swing door at the side of the courtroom and stepped into the dock. Richard turned to give him a reassuring smile which was met with an expression of acute wariness.

The clerk frowned at a piece of paper in front of him.

"Are one of you gentlemen representing Butcher?" he asked, glancing cursorily at the assembled lawyers,

111

"I am," Richard said, getting up.

"Mr. Monk, is it?" His tone was almost insolent in its determination to show he had no favourites.

"It is."

"Very well." He looked to where Detective-Inspector Drew had stepped forward from a throng of police officers. "You have an application, Inspector?"

"Yes, your Worships," Drew said from the threshold of the witness-box. "I'm asking for a remand in custody for seven days. The police have a great many further inquiries to make and the case is one which has to be referred to the Director of Public Prosecutions."

"When will you be ready to go ahead?" the clerk inquired briskly.

"I'm not in a position to say that today, sir. Anyway, it'll depend on the Director of Public Prosecutions."

"Very well." He turned and addressed the chairman of the magistrates. "As you've heard, sir, the application is for a seven-day remand in custody."

"I'd like to say something, sir," Richard said, standing up and looking faintly pugnacious.

The clerk threw him the look he reserved specially for lawyers who were strangers to his court and whom he promptly stigmatised as potential nuisances. It was a look compounded of intolerance and irritation.

"Well, what is it?"

Ostentatiously ignoring him and addressing himself to the three magistrates Richard said, "I'm sure I don't need to remind you, sir, that the defence also have rights in this matter. You're not there merely to endorse whatever the police ask for, as I'm sure your learned clerk will agree." He managed to inject a subtle amount of scorn into the word *learned* and noted the effect with satisfaction. The clerk scowled furiously. "I'm not objecting to this remand, sir," he went on. "It would be unreasonable to do so. The point I am making, however, is that the defence would like the hearing to take place as soon as possible, and we certainly won't be willing to go on concurring in indefinite delay while the police, to use Inspector Drew's own words, make their great many further inquiries." He cast a challenging look around him. "I thought I should make that quite clear at the outset, sir. After all, the police are presumably satisfied they have sufficient evidence or they wouldn't have charged my client in the first place. So there can't be any good reason for delaying the hearing."

He sat down, while the clerk continued for several seconds to stare ahead of him with a heavy scowl. Then with a meaningful sniff and a freezing glance at Richard, he turned round and whispered to the chairman, who, with his two colleagues had assumed expressions of studied detachment while Richard had been addressing them.

The colloquy over, the chairman said, "We remand the accused in custody for seven days. We hope the police will take note of Mr. Monk's remarks and we shall certainly not be prepared, for our part, to countenance any undue delay in the hearing of this case."

In the jostle to get out of court which followed, Richard found himself next to Inspector Drew who said to him reproachfully, "You certainly didn't make things any easier, Mr. Monk."

"I could say the same to you, Inspector," he replied with a half-smile. "But if the police will rush in and charge people with crimes before they've assembled all the evidence, this situation inevitably arises."

Drew shook his head sorrowfully. "I know. It's the system," he murmured. "Incidentally, you know who that was sitting next to you?"

"Caspar's solicitor."

"Yes. What did you think of him?"

"An eight-cylinder, twin-carburettor smoothie."

Drew chuckled. "Come across him before?"

"No, have you?"

"Not personally. Heard about him though. Gather he rakes it in. The money, I mean."

"What about the clerk?"

"He's all right."

"For whom?"

This exchange had brought them into the jailer's office and Richard was taken along to the cells to have a word with Eddie.

"Sorry I couldn't speak to you beforehand, but I got terribly held up driving down and arrived only just in time."

"That's all right. You made up for it afterwards," Eddie replied easily. "I liked the way you put that little shit of a clerk in his place." His mood of elation was short-lived, however, and his expression became drawn and anxious. "Brixton's really getting on my tits. I'm in a hospital ward with a lot of nut cases. The only thing they worry about is having enough cigs to smoke." His tone became vehement, "I'd never have come back if I'd known, I was crazy. I could have lived in ease for the rest of my days. Instead I had to return to England and walk slap into this."

"Aren't you forgetting why you did come back?"

"Diane, you mean? A fat lot of hope I've got of seeing her again?"

I can't be mistaken, Richard thought to himself, I'm sure he's genuine. I'm sure he didn't murder Paula Caspar. But did he, perhaps, as was suggested, intend to murder Caspar? No! The answer to one must be the answer to the other.

"You've got a funny look on your face, Mr. Monk."

"Er . . . sorry. I was thinking."

"Must have been disturbing thoughts."

Richard ignored the comment. He could hardly say, "Well, as a matter of fact I was wondering whether you're guilty despite your protestations to the contrary."

"Was there anyone in Court you recognised?" he asked in a brisk tone.

"Caspar's solicitor, sitting next to you. And I had a glimpse of Jack Ebony at the back just as I was going out. Caspar himself certainly wasn't there."

"That's not surprising." A silence followed during which, for several seconds, Eddie glared at the cell wall, then his face slowly crumpled and he began to cry. Richard gazed at him in mute bewilderment.

17

Richard drove back to London with his mind in more of a turmoil than it had been on the journey down.

Eddie's break-down had surprised him completely. It would never have occurred to him that a man who had lived on his wits for years in a society about as secure as a barrel of dynamite could become so suddenly forlorn and sunk in tearful despair. He had pulled himself together quickly enough, but had offered no conventional apology for his embarrassing display of unmasculine emotion. The small maggot of doubt in Richard's mind gave a squirm. Had it all been a calculated display to win his sympathy?

He let out a groan. Why had fate sent Eddie Butcher across his path? Why had each of them have to be in Japan at the same moment?

Japan! He thought over what had happened in Kyoto and during those final days in Tokyo. The attempt on Eddie's life, his own curious meeting with Miss Shima at the café in Shinjuku. Those two events were surely sufficient proof of Caspar's evil? But that wasn't what he entertained any doubts about! Neither of them assisted in any way resolving the uncertainty he had begun to feel about his own client. He started at the other end and tried to analyse what it was in the first place which had given him belief in Eddie Butcher's cause.

Driving the car, however, required too much of his concentration and he found that his thought were merely going round in full circles.

He gave up. He envied Mr. Haymore Jarvis who could have no such worrying doubts about his client. *He* knew exactly where he stood. *His* client was a hundred per cent crook and, furthermore, he aided and abetted him in his crookery.

At more or less the same moment that Richard's thoughts turned to Mr. Jarvis, that gentleman was on the telephone to Caspar.

"I didn't much care for Monk's attitude," he said. "I think he could give us a bit of trouble. We certainly needn't expect any co-operation from that quarter."

"Perhaps not *voluntary* co-operation," Caspar murmured.

"He wasn't inclined to tell me everything," Mr. Jarvis went on, "not even on a lawyer to lawyer basis. He'll be a fighter all the way."

"What's he look like?"

"Medium height. Compactly built. Short, curlyish hair. Slightly worried expression which vanishes when he smiles. He has a nice smile."

"I'm happy to know he gave you one."

"Not me. I saw him smiling afterwards when he was talking to Inspector Drew₂"

Caspar's tone became suddenly sharp. "What the hell's Drew got anything to smile about with the defence lawyer?"

"Jack's with me, Ralph," Mr. Jarvis said quickly. "He'd like to have a word with you."

"I got a good look at Butcher," Ebony said, taking the receiver which the solicitor had thrust at him.

"How was he?"

"Worried. Definitely worried."

"That's nothing to what he's going to be."

Caspar's tone held a note of anticipation and relish which caused even Ebony to prickle at the top of his spine. It was rare for the boss to reveal that sort of emotion, but Paula's death had obviously hit him hard.

"Nothing," Caspar added before he abruptly rang off.

18

Like all good secretaries, Sheila Gillam was adept at protecting her employer from unwanted telephone calls. She had all the usual stalling ploys at her command; nevertheless, like only the best of the good secretaries, she had that sixth sense which told her when to put through to Richard a caller whom she would normally have fought off—but for that extra sense.

So it came about that the next morning, not long after he'd arrived in his office, Richard's phone gave one of its short, discreet buzzes and he lifted the receiver to hear Sheila's voice.

"There's a Mr. Poultney on the line who wants to speak to you, Mr. Monk," she said. "He won't tell me anything about himself, but he says he's quite sure you'll be interested in what he has to say."

"And I gather you think so, too?"

"Yes, something tells me you ought to speak to him yourself."

"You'd better put him through then."

The line went dead for a second or two before the connection was made.

"Am I speaking to Mr. Richard Monk?"

"Monk speaking," Richard replied, wincing slightly at the falsely unctuous tone of his mysterious caller.

"My name is Poultney, Albert Poultney. I'm a private inquiry agent, Mr. Monk, and I was recently employed by the late Mrs. Caspar."

"Ah!"

"Yes, I thought that would interest you, Mr. Monk. I always believe in coming to the point straight away and not wasting people's time. Especially that of busy professional men like yourself."

He paused after making this little speech, clearly waiting for Richard to bite more deeply on the bait.

"Assuming my interest, Mr. Poultney, go ahead."

Mr. Poultney appeared to chuckle. "I like your forthrightness, Mr. Monk, but perhaps there are one or two small details

117

we ought to clear out of the way first."

"Such as?"

"Mr. Monk, I can tell that you're a man after my own heart. You don't like beating about the bush any more than I do, so I'll put my cards on the table. I can't do fairer than that, can I, Mr. Monk?"

"No," Richard replied with an exasperated glance at the ceiling, "you certainly can't."

"Now I know we understand each other, Mr. Monk," Mr. Poultney said in a richly bonhomous tone. "Quite frankly, Mr. Monk, I'm in a slightly embarrassing position. I was, as I've already mentioned, employed on a confidential assignment by the late Mrs. Caspar. Now the poor lady has passed on and the assignment remains uncompleted. She, rest her soul, has no further interest, of course, in the completion of the task she entrusted me with. On the other hand, it seems such a very great pity, if I may say so, that so much work should be wasted when, if I may be so bold, its successful completion might be of very considerable interest to your good self, I mean, of course, in your capacity as defender of the unfortunate young man who has been charged with Mrs. Caspar's murder."

"How does Mr. Caspar fit in with this assignment you refer to?" Richard asked cautiously.

"A very pertinent question, Mr. Monk. A very pertinent question, indeed. How shall I answer it now! Let me just say that Mr. Caspar was totally unaware of my assignment, but at the same time very much part of it. I trust you won't think I'm answering you in riddles."

"What you're telling me is that Mrs. Caspar was paying you to find out something about her husband? Is that it?"

"In a nutshell, Mr. Monk. In a nutshell," Mr. Poultney observed delightedly.

"And what was the something?"

"You go so fast, Mr. Monk, I have difficulty in keeping up with you. We really have now reached the stage when we must pause and strike our bargain. Don't think, dear sir, that I'm not trusting you. If I may say so, your voice alone is a passport of your integrity. And anyway, as we both know, honour is never a problem between professional men; though I trust that I'm not presuming in referring to myself as a professional man."

"Mr. Poultney," Richard said firmly, "I think you're inviting me, on behalf of my client, to pay you to complete the

118

assignment on which you were working for Mrs. Caspar. I might very well be prepared to do that, but obviously I must first know something about the nature of the assignment. Only then can I tell you whether we can reach an agreement."

"Very succinctly put, if I may say so, dear sir. Exactly what I would have expected from a man of your high professional reputation. Makes things so much easier dealing with such a person. Would that all my clients were as honest and forthright..."

"Mr. Poultney!" Richard's tone held a warning note which was not lost on his caller.

"Yes, Mr. Monk, I agree it's time we came to the point. Mrs. Caspar suspected—and suspected with good reason, let me say —that her husband was being unfaithful to her and she employed my good services to find out who the other woman was. There, now I've given it to you in a nutshell."

"But you've not yet identified her?"

"Not quite yet, but I was hot on the scent when the tragedy struck. I have no hesitation in guaranteeing success, however, should you be interested..."

"Just tell me two things, Mr. Poultney. Do you know the use to which Mrs. Caspar was going to put the information? I mean, was she seeking grounds for divorce?"

"She didn't confide in me to that extent, Mr. Monk, but I ... er, I couldn't help forming my own impression. No, I don't think she was interested in divorce..."

"What then?"

"I think she may have wanted the information as a sort of lever against her husband."

"Blackmail, you mean?"

"Tch, tch! That's not a word I like to use over the telephone," Mr. Poultney said reprovingly.

"I see! And you're quite certain Mr. Caspar had no inkling that he was under your surveillance?"

"I'm a professional, Mr. Monk, not a bungling amateur," Mr. Poultney replied with dignity. "I don't stand about on draughty street corners, drawing attention to myself, with my coat collar turned up and my hat pulled down."

Richard forebore to point out that Caspar was also a professional and one, moreover, who presumably took great pains to ensure that nobody found out more about him that he wanted known. Perhaps, however, the very fact that Mr. Poultney was still in one piece did confirm that he hadn't been detected. From the beginning of their conversation, Richard had not been in any doubt as to what his answer would be. If Mr. Poultney could successfully complete his task, the result might be of the greatest possible significance to Eddie's defence. And even if he didn't complete it, there was value in what he'd already discovered. The more he thought about it, the greater he saw Mr. Poultney's potential as a defence witness.

"O.K. Mr. Poultney, it's a deal. What are your terms?"

There followed a further five minutes of dialogue during which Mr. Poultney emphasised the difficulties and dangers of the particular assignment. "I'm sure I don't need to tell you, Mr. Monk, what sort of a man Ralph Caspar is. It couldn't be a more delicate or hazardous assignment if I were keeping one of the top men in Cosa Nostra under observation."

Eventually terms were agreed and Mr. Poultney was given two weeks to come up with something worth while. Richard made a mental reservation that he would be prepared to extend this time limit if the situation justified, but he had no intention of letting Mr. Poultney know this in advance. As it was, he could see himself being led on—and on— and on, always with the promise of success round the corner, and he had been at pains to disabuse Mr. Poultney's mind in advance against being tempted along this path. Mr. Poultney was not the first private inquiry agent with whom he had had dealings, even if he was the fondest user of evasive platitudes.

"I gather from the length of the call that I did right in putting Mr. Poultney through" Sheila said when she came into his room a few minutes later to take dictation.

Richard grinned. "I believe you know by the pricking of your thumbs, same as a witch."

"Is there any other way?" she inquired.

After Sheila had retired to her own room again, he fell to further contemplation of Eddie's defence. And the more he thought about it, the more clearly he realised that it could only consist of a formal attack on Caspar. Caspar would have to be so discredited that a jury could not begin to accept his word. This meant that the more ammunition he could find to use against Caspar, the better. So strength to Mr. Poultney! All allies welcome!

It was half way through the afternoon when Sheila stuck her head round the door and said, "There's a Miss Paisley downstairs who'd like to see you."

Richard looked up keenly. "Well, well! what a day this is

proving to be for unexpected callers! Have her sent up."

Diane Paisley looked pale and anxious as she sat down in the chair which Richard offered her. There were circles beneath her eyes. She glanced distractedly around her as though unsure that she had done the right thing in coming. All this Richard took in as he held out the cigarette box which he kept for his visitors. She accepted one and began fumbling in her bag for a light before she realised he had picked up his desk lighter. She had rather a sallow complexion and large brown eyes which were shy and grave and determined all at the same time. Her hair hung short and straight from a centre parting and she wore it in a fringe over her forehead.

"I'm afraid you won't have the faintest idea who I am," she said, after inhaling deeply and letting the smoke drift slowly away from her.

"On the contrary, Miss Paisley, I know exactly who you are." She frowned at him suspiciously. "I also have a fairly good idea why you've called to see me."

"Please explain how you know about me?"

"I met your friend Eddie Butcher when we were both in Japan recently and he talked quite a lot about you."

"Did he tell you everything?" she asked incredulously,

"I would imagine he probably did," Richard said. "He certainly told me of his friendship with you and how you wouldn't accompany him abroad."

Her expression became suddenly bleak. "And did he tell you why I wouldn't?"

"Yes."

"Then perhaps you know everything . . ." Her voice trailed away, overtaken by thoughts which Richard could only guess at.

"Have you come to see me because you want to help him?"

She nodded. "Ever since I heard of his arrest, I've been wondering what to do. And then when I saw your name in the paper and that you were defending him. I made up my mind to come to London and see you." As she finished speaking, she gave an involuntary shiver and glanced quickly toward the window. "Caspar threatened me to stay away from London," she explained. "I'm afraid I'm still feeling a bit scared at having defied him."

"Where've you been since you left London?" Richard asked.

"In Lincolnshire," she said, and went on to give him a resumé of her own existence from the time when she and Eddie had finally parted. When she had finished, she put up a finger to remove the tear which was poised on her cheekbone.

Richard looked at her with compassion. "It may help if I tell you that Eddie came back solely on your account."

"Is that really true?" she asked eagerly.

He nodded. "I've no doubt he'll tell you so himself when you go and see him."

"May I really do that?" Her eyes were shining and she swallowed back the emotion which was threatening to choke her.

"Yes, you certainly may. There are no restrictions on his visitors while he's on remand." He paused and frowned. "On the other hand, I think we must be a bit careful about this. I wouldn't put it beyond Caspar's powers to check on Eddie's visitors. From all I gather, he has a pretty effective intelligence network and I can't help feeling that it stretches into prisons. Anyway, you can certainly go and visit him. What I'll do is arrange for you to be driven there and back and I'll see that you have a driver who knows if he's being followed and, more to the point, knows how to shake off a tail. Where are you going to stay in London?"

"I don't know."

"We'll fix that up, too, before you leave." He leaned forward, resting his clasped hands on the edge of the desk. "And now I want to ask you something really important," he said seriously. "During the whole of your disagreeable interview with Caspar, did you see or hear anything which might be used to discredit him? Think back very carefully over everything that happened while you were at his flat."

For half a minute Diane stared ahead of her, chin slightly jutted out and lips parted. Then with a little shake, she turned her gaze to Richard.

"It's curious what fear does to your recollection" she said slowly. "I can remember some things as vividly as if they'd been tattooed on my mind with a red hot needle and others are no more than faint shadows. I'll never forget their three faces," she said vehemently. "And I could still describe to you exactly how each one was dressed." She gave another small shake of the head as though by doing so one memory would dissolve and a fresh one take its place. "Finally, after I broke down and told them that Eddie was making for Japan, they lost interest in me for a little while. They'd got what they wanted out of me. I was sitting huddled at one end of the sofa and they were talking amongst themselves. I think it was

the short one of the two—that would be Ebony, wouldn't it?
—anyway, I think it was he who said something like, 'Of
course, he'll still believe Shima is your chap there, Ralph.'
And Caspar nodded and said, 'That won't be his only surprise.
I'll call Fukiko and tell him to remove Eddie as effectively as
he removed Shima.' "

Richard nodded keenly. "Can you remember any other
snatches of conversation?"

"I remember how Tendo—he's the big blond thuggish one—
laughed when Caspar said that and added something like,
'Fukiko'll make him wish he'd committed hara kiri.' "

"This may be important," Richard said. "but you're certain
Caspar said something to the effect that Fukiko would be in-
structed to remove Eddie in the same way he'd removed
Shima?"

"It was definitely something like that. I may have got the
Japanese names a bit wrong, but I don't think so. For some
crazy reason they've stuck in my mind. Probably because my
sub-conscious was surprised at hearing three such unlikely
people bandying about Japanese names."

Richard nodded. His own mind had gone back to his meeting with Miss Shima on his last day in Tokyo. It seemed that
he would, after all, have something to tell her about her
brother's mysterious disappearance and death. What was more,
the present day had brought a supply of much needed ammunition for use against Caspar. With the promise of yet
more to come.

"What you've told me, Miss Paisley, is tremendously important," he said.

"You think it'll help Eddie?"

"Yes, I do." A frown passed across his face. "But it'll mean
a considerable ordeal for you, because you'll have to stand up
and give it as evidence in court. Will you be prepared to do
that?"

She bit nervously at her lower lip, then said quietly, "Yes,
It's the least I can do for Eddie."

19

Paula Caspar's funeral attracted all the attention of a film première or a public hanging. Large crowds, mostly of middle-aged women, thronged the approaches to the crematorium and stared with ferocious intensity at every coming and going, which was followed by ripples of comment, for the most part ill-informed, and occasionally pungently so. The majority had been drawn by that deep-seated yearning to participate vicariously in all the morbid associations of a spectacular funeral.

Also there in force were the Press and police. Inspector Drew had felt reluctantly obliged to be present when he learned that a number of his colleagues, interested in various aspects of Caspar's activities, were proposing to attend.

The actual mourners themselves represented a mere handful of those who filled the small chapel. Ralph Caspar's neat, over-coated figure stood slightly apart from the others. From where Inspector Drew was standing he looked smaller, and even shrunken, but perhaps this was imagination—or perhaps people did physically shrink in such circumstances. Drew's mind recalled the picture of his own mother standing at his father's graveside and how she had suddenly seemed to have become lost inside her clothes.

In the front pew on the opposite side of the aisle from Caspar were Tony Tendo and Jack Ebony with their wives. The wives were dressed entirely in black and Tendo wore a black crêpe band on his right sleeve in addition to a black tie and black socks.

"Ours is the biggest wreath, Bridge," he whispered in a pleased tone to his wife. "I had a look at them all just before we came in."

Bridget Tendo received the information with an uninterested nod. Her gaze was fixed on the coffin lying on the cata-falque only a few feet from them and waiting to be slid from their sight through a hatch in the chapel wall. A single green wreath rested on it with a card bearing the inscription: "To my beloved Paula from your ever-loving Ralph."

It was a large card and the handwriting upon it was large too, so that nobody had to strain in order to read what was written.

Bridget Tendo hated funerals. They dried up all her emotion and left her feeling like a husk of her real self. And this one was worse than most in that respect. She was no more religious than her husband, but he had the capacity which she lacked of being emotionally stirred on such an occasion. She hadn't the slightest doubt that as the coffin disappeared from final view, he would pull out his handkerchief and blow his nose loudly to cover his choked emotions. All she could do was just stare hypnotically at Paula's boxed-up remains, now silently awaiting the flames of final destruction. She felt suffocated by the black she was wearing and the thought that she had surrendered to conformity dried her up even further inside. She stole a quick glance along the row at the other three. Marie Ebony had a faraway expression of boredom and her husband, Jack, was staring ahead of him with a set frown. Tony, her own husband, was fingering the outsize knot of his tie and looked like a small boy about to make his first acquaintance with Santa Claus.

At last it was all over and they came out into lukewarm sunshine. Caspar stood on the step of the chapel, looking faintly bewildered. Mr. Haymore Jarvis came up to him.

"Let's get away from here," he muttered. "All these morbid onlookers give me the willies."

Caspar glanced at him and frowned.

"Whose funeral is this!" he said coldly.

"I'm sorry, Ralph," the solicitor said, hastily. "I didn't mean to upset you. I was only thinking of you. I thought you'd like to get away as soon as possible."

"I'll leave when I'm ready. But no one's stopping you."

Caspar moved a few yards over to where Inspector Drew was surveying the scene with an expression of dubiety.

"Good afternoon, Inspector." Drew nodded a formal greeting. "I can't believe that it's respect for the memory of my late wife which has brought you here. Or others of your colleagues whom I seem to recognise."

"No, that's right," Drew said stolidly. Then, feeling that he had been blunter than the occasion required, he added. "I'm afraid I never met your wife, but a policeman's duty is apt to take him to all manner of unlikely places, even to funerals."

"What were you hoping to find out?" Caspar inquired.

"Nothing in particular. I just came to see who else was here."

"I hope you found it rewarding."

"Not really," Drew replied with truth.

"Are you satisfied that you have a strong enough case against Butcher?"

"Strong enough?"

"To convict him."

"You can never tell with an English jury. They go on instinct as much as evidence."

"Look, Inspector," Caspar said in a quietly vicious tone, "that man murdered my wife all right, and I don't want the police to pull any punches."

"I'm shocked to hear you even suggest such a thing."

"You're either a knave or a hypocrite, Inspector. But let me make my position quite clear. If I have any reason to believe that you've not done everything you should have in investigating this case; that the evidence falls short because of some failure on your part, then I shall make such a protest that you won't see your precious pension rights for the smouldering ruins of your career." His tone had never risen above a conversational level and he now added in the same quietly dispassionate tone, "That's not an idle threat. It's a promise, which I can and will fulfill, so let there be no misunderstanding."

At least half a dozen replies passed through Drew's mind, but he deemed it politic to voice none of them, or he'd have played straight into Caspar's hands. It was one of those occasions for stoical silence that a police officer is trained to recognise.

"And while we're talking to one another, there's something else," Caspar went on in the same hard, even tone. "The investigation of my wife's murder is no call to the police to inquire into my life as a whole, nor to keep a watch on my movements. I shall resist vigorously any attempt to carry this inquiry outside its proper limits. And now that you've made an arrest, those limits are even narrower than they were before. So keep your nose out of my affairs and tell your friends in the Fraud and Flying Squads to do likewise, or I'll see that they burn their fingers badly."

"Their noses were long, but it was their fingers which got burnt," Drew said in a musing tone.

"Restrict your cleverness to that sort of remark," Caspar retorted, "and you'll be all right." He turned on his heel and walked across to the black Rolls Royce whose rear door was being held open by a uniformed chauffeur. A few seconds later he was being driven slowly through the still patiently waiting throng outside the gate. Heads craned to catch a glimpse of him, and one woman hopefully held out an autograph book.

Inspector Drew watched until the car had turned out of sight. He felt like someone caught in a rock-crushing machine. Seldom, if ever had he had a case in which duty and inclination were in such open conflict. But it was worse than this, for, at the same time as they were in conflict, they merged into one. The problem was of knowing how far he was justified in widening the scope of his investigation. What was very clear to him was that he could come in for criticism in the course of the trial both for doing too much and for doing too little.

He could clearly hear the cold, judicial voice intoning its condemnation. "For some reason best known to themselves the police have seen fit not to inquire into this extremely pertinent aspect of the case . . ." or "The police seem to have thought that they had a license to probe matters, which by no stretch even of their lively imaginations could have been of possible relevance to the issues we're here concerned with . . ."

He sighed and gave a small, helpless shrug as he walked off in search of his own car;

20

The next two weeks passed without any overt developments. It was as though those concerned in the forthcoming trial had gone into secret training for the event.

Richard paid a number of visits to Eddie in Brixton Prison to discuss his defence and each time found him in good spirits. He realised that this was not a flattering comment on his own morale-raising qualities, but was due entirely to the rapprochement between Eddie and Diane. She had been to see him regularly and he, for his part, obviously felt that his return to England had been vindicated by her present support. Indeed, Richard, who had been the witness of this affecting reconciliation, had felt obliged to remind each that there were still a very large number of imponderables strewn ahead. Otherwise he feared that they might be carried away by the romantic notion that love solves everything and, in particular, that the love of a good woman reduces murder charges to the equivalent of petty larceny.

"We'll certainly put up a tough fight," he had said to Eddie on one of his visits to Brixton, "and we'll hurl everything we can lay hands on at Caspar, but I don't want you to get over-confident."

"What do you think my chances are?" Eddie had asked eagerly.

Richard had shaken his head. "Sorry, but that's not the sort of question I'm prepared to try to answer."

"Fifty, fifty? Sixty, forty?"

"Look! Criminal trials are not conducted according to mathematical patterns, which all lead up to a single answer you can see clearly set out at the bottom of the page. That's not the way verdicts are reached. I'm afraid they're much more a process of gurgitation. You feed bits of evidence to the jury and they chew on them and decide what they think of the taste, whether they think it's overdone or underdone, whether it's fresh or synthetic, and, in the final analysis, whether they find it digestible or indigestible. That's the way juries reach

128

verdicts."

"And what the hell is the judge doing all this time?"

"He may sprinkle a bit of his own pepper and salt on the evidence if he thinks he ought to make it more palatable. Equally, he's not above trying to make it inedible. In your case, everything will hinge on the impression which Caspar makes on the jury. *Everything*."

It was on this visit, too, that he had returned to Eddie and said, "Why did you choose Japan to go to? I suspect you've never told me the true reason."

Eddie gave a resigned shrug. "I thought I might be able to strike a deal with Shima and muscle in on some of Caspar's interests there. I think I told you we took a bit of a fancy to one another when he came to England. But I discovered when I got to Tokyo that Shima had disappeared and Caspar had a new man looking after things for him. A much tougher chap, who clearly had orders to kill me, as Diane has since confirmed." His mouth twisted into a smile. "And that's why I went to Japan."

"I'd guessed as much," Richard said. "but thanks for answering my question. I had wondered if that was the real reason. It didn't otherwise seem quite your sort of country."

This conversation had taken place a few days before the hearing in the Magistrates' Court which resulted in Eddie being committed for trial at the Assizes. The prosecution called about eight witnesses, of whom Ralph Caspar was by far the most important. He gave his evidence in a quiet, even tone and displayed none of the emotional chinks in his armour which an opposing advocate might be able to exploit with profit. Provided a jury knew nothing about him at all, he would go down well. On the other hand Richard and Alan Scarby would ensure that they knew a great deal about him before he left the witness box. Mud-slinging, though, was a hazardous operation, not only on account of what might be slung back, but, once more, because of the jury factor. Those so-called twelve good men and true were quite capable of becoming suddenly repelled and of abruptly switching their sympathies from the mud thrower to his target.

What Richard did notice, however, as he watched Caspar in the witness box in the Magistrates' Court, were the signs of physical ordeal. He looked like someone who hadn't had a good night's sleep for weeks. The expression remained impassive but there was anything but impassivity behind it, Richard reckoned.

On this occasion, he had contrived to ensure that the D.P.P.'s representative sat between himself and Mr. Haymore Jarvis. He had cross-examined a number of the prosecution witnesses, so that the atmosphere in court was electric when prosecuting council sat down on completion of his examination-in-chief of Caspar.

Mr. Jarvis fixed him with a steely stare and Ebony and Tendo both craned forward in their seats at the back. The Press shifted themselves into fresh postures of attention.

Richard stood up and waited for complete silence before announcing with full dramatic effect, "Cross-examination of this witness is reserved." His tone seemed to say, as he intended it should, that the defence had a whole range of secret missiles at their disposal and that these would be discharged at the right time—namely at the trial. Until then, let everyone speculate—and Caspar in particular.

"What's he up to?" Tendo whispered uneasily to Ebony.

"He's not asking Ralph any questions in this court. That's what he's up to, the crafty little bastard!"

"But why? I don't follow."

"He's not going to give anything away in advance, that's what it means. If he asked questions here, we'd know the lines of Butcher's defence. But he's not going to give us that pleasure."

"I don't trust him," Tendo remarked darkly.

"You're bloody right not to trust him. Didn't you hear Jarvis say he'd been making some inquiries and that he was one of the astutest criminal lawyers in town?"

"Perhaps we could use him ourselves."

Their conversation was terminated at this point by one of the police officers on duty tapping Tendo on the shoulder from behind and saying, "Either keep quiet or get out."

"Who the hell are you talking to?" Tendo muttered angrily.

"I know exactly who I'm talking to," the officer replied with a note of grim relish.

One of the reasons Ebony and Tendo had come to court was to see if Diane turned up. She hadn't—on Richard's instructions—and this had been a disappointment. They had learnt of her visits to Brixton Prison, but such had been Richard's security arrangements that they'd not been able to do anything about it, least of all trail her to an address. As it happened, she was staying at the home of Sheila Gillam's mother who lived in Putney. It was a sensible arrangement which Sheila herself had proposed, and Richard was duly grateful to his secretary for such a practical suggestion.

The Assizes to which Eddie was committed for trial were due to begin in three weeks' time. With the Magistrates' Court hearing over, everyone retired once more into their own corners to prepare for the major round ahead.

It was about ten days later that Sheila came through on Richard's extension late one afternoon and said a trifle wearily, "It's Mr. Poultney again. He says it's something important. But he says that every time. Do you want to speak to him? I told him I wasn't sure if you were in your room, so you don't have to."

Mr. Poultney had been in the habit of telephoning Richard every third or fourth day with a progress report. Except that it amounted to a non-progress report, once stripped of all the attendant circumlocution. It appeared that Caspar was being even more discreet than before. Either that or, as Richard was beginning to suspect, Mr. Poultney's efficiency didn't match his hopeful forecasts. At all events, he had begun to think in terms of withdrawing Mr. Poultney's instructions, since his further employment seemed to be a waste of money. This would be as good a moment as any to tell him so. He had twice extended the time limit given him and Mr. Poultney probably reckoned that this would go on indefinitely. Well, he was about to learn otherwise.

"No, put him through, I'd like to have a word with him," Richard said a trifle grimly.

"Good afternoon there, Mr. Monk, I have some news which I think will interest you." This was his traditional opening and it did nothing but increase Richard's determination to be shot of the cloying old scoundrel. He was tired of all the soft soap. "Yes, something rather curious has happened. Indeed, I might say *very* curious. I'm not sure what to make of it. I think probably the best thing would be for me to come and see you. Pay you a visit in your sumptuous domain."

"Get to the point, Mr. Poultney, and tell me what the curious thing is that's happened."

"Get to the point, how right you are, Mr. Monk! That's what I'm always trying to instill into my young assistant. Get to the point, Raymond, I'm constantly saying to him, nobody wants to listen to all your blather about *how* you discovered what you did. They want to know *what* you discovered. It's your findings that count, Raymond, I say to him, not the process by which you arrived at them."

"Mr. Poultney!" Richard barked.

"So if you'll allow me, Mr. Monk, I'd like to come to the point." He cleared his throat portentiously. "I've received a communication which seems to indicate that someone else is interested in my inquiry into Mr. Caspar's *other* life. Someone apart from your good self, that is."

"Tell me more."

"Ah! I thought I should secure your interest, Mr. Monk," he said roguishly. "It's only a short note and it's unsigned, but that isn't the only thing which is curious about it. Indeed, I suppose its lack of signature is one of the least curious things about it. No, one of the more curious things about it is that it has come from across the water. It appears that there is someone in Japan who is interested in Mr. Caspar's love-life."

"Japan!"

"Japan, Mr. Monk. To be more precise, Tokyo. That's the postmark on the envelope. Tokyo where all those lovely Geisha girls give all the tired men such a treat."

Richard raised his eyes to the ceiling in silent prayer. Pictures of the Ginza, South American waterfronts, Montmartre, and Hamburg's Reeperbahn, were, he suspected, all stored away in the more prurient half of Mr. Poultney's mind.

"But the most curious thing of all about this communication," Mr. Poultney now went on, " . . . well, this is really what I think I ought to come and see you about, Mr. Monk. When would be convenient for me to call?"

"You'd better come straight away," Richard said.

"Splendid, Mr. Monk. You really are a man after my own heart. Action and promptness, those are the qualities I like in a man. I'll be around in twenty minutes."

Richard waited with burning impatience for his arrival. He felt mystified and intrigued. Above all, however, he had a tingling sensation at the top of his spine that told him something dramatic was in the offing.

It was exactly twenty minutes later that Sheila announced on the phone, "Mr. Poultney's arrived and is on his way up . . ."

21

Richard gazed down on the North Pole with that sense of euphoric unreality that long hours of flying induce. It was only just seventy-two hours ago that Mr. Poultney had made the telephone call, followed by his visit to Richard's office, which in turn led to the series of hectic discussions and conferences with Alan Scarby, of which the present journey to Tokyo was the outcome.

Adjustable instrument though Richard's mind usually was, he was feeling dazed by the pace at which everything had happened. A pace, nevertheless, that he himself had generated. He hadn't had time during those three days, once the decision had been taken, to give his mind to anything other than the immediate plans for his journey. Now, suspended in a warm cocoon six miles above the top of the world, there was time to reflect and see the venture in better perspective. Except that it wasn't a better perspective. Before, he may have been too close to the events he was fashioning, now he was too far removed from them. His whole existence seemed absurdly unimportant viewed from his present position. Moreover, it was pretentious to think otherwise.

He felt like a drug addict who knows that the dreamlike effect will wear off, but can meanwhile only surrender to it. With this conclusion pigeon-holed in his mind, he closed his eyes and drowsily contemplated what would happen if the plane had to make a forced landing on the North Pole . . . The next thing he knew they had made a scheduled landing in Alaska.

It was six o'clock in the evening when they taxied up to the terminal at Tokyo International Airport. Richard didn't know what evening, nor did he care. He took a cab to his hotel, had a shower, a complete change of clothing, and two glasses of delicious cold beer, after all of which he felt civilised again.

He had decided to stay at a different hotel from his previous visit and he had also taken care not to give anyone advance notice of his arrival.

As he stood enjoying his second glass of beer and gazing out of the window at the rain-swept landscape, he tried to decide what his order of priorities should be and whether he should tackle the first this very evening or give himself a night's sleep and start fresh in the morning.

While he was thus reviewing his thoughts, there was a knock on the door and a beaming young man came in with the request that he might turn down the bed. Richard watched the quick, deft movements with which he worked and acknowledged the formal bow he received on completion of the job. It was pleasant to be back in a country where personal service really did come with a smile.

He drained the glass and stood for a while still gazing out of the window. The scene was one which he had come to regard as typically Tokyo. There was the ubiquitous Tower looking like an enlarged version of the one at Blackpool, clusters of modern blocks surmounted by flashing neon, and in the immediate foreground a huddle of grey wooden houses, each in a leafy garden and with a narrow lane winding through their midst. Closer still an artificial waterfall splashed down into an ornamental pool, unabashed by nature's own plentiful contribution at that moment.

Richard turned from the scene and picked up his raincoat. It was time to go. He'd flown to Japan for a specific purpose. Let him get on with it.

A taxi pulled forward as he came out of the hotel entrance. He was about to open the rear door when it sprang at him. Of course! He'd never become used to Tokyo taxi drivers being able to operate the doors from their own seat. He gave the driver the name of a hotel and sat back. Another thing he hadn't got used to with Tokyo taxi drivers was their youth. Some of them looked hardly old enough to hold licences, but they drove with all the reckless verve of veterans in this most competitive of occupations.

The hotel to which Richard was driven was one of several built in time for the 1964 Olympics. It was ultra-modern with an uneasy blend of western style and Japanese trimmings. A bit like a new rich man's dream home, Richard thought as he entered and looked somewhat cautiously around him.

The lobby presented the cosmopolitan scene increasingly repeated round the world in the jet age. Within half a minute, Richard had heard English, French, German and an unidentified language being spoken, in addition to Japanese.

At the far side of the lobby, shallow steps led down between four blood-red Roman pillars into a large semi-circular lounge, which was furnished in various shades of grey. He walked across and stood for a moment beside one of the pillars. He wasn't sure what he expected to find in the lounge, but it was certainly not what in fact met his eyes. Over in a far corner, sitting on one of the sofas were a man and a woman. The woman he had never seen before in his life. But the man he had. It was Ralph Caspar.

22

Thank God for the plump, blood-red pillars, Richard thought, as he stepped smartly behind one of them.

For several seconds he stood staring vacantly across the lobby with his back to the protective pillar while his thoughts, which had become momentarily atomised, began slowly to coalesce again.

Caspar in Tokyo! What on earth was he doing here? A question, however, which required no second asking after a moment's reflection.

There was a bench seat in a small alcove a few paces away. It was unoccupied and he went across and sat in it. He found that if he squeezed himself up at one end, he could see round the curve of one of the pillars to where Caspar and the woman were sitting. It was equally certain that the pillars and two tier lay-out of the lobby would prevent their spotting him. In any event, Caspar had his back half-turned toward Richard and the woman, who was more or less facing his direction, wouldn't know him from Adam.

She was sitting very still with her hands folded in her lap while Caspar seemed to be doing all the talking. Her expression remained blank, apart from an occasional blinking of her eyes as she refocussed her attention.

For two or three minutes, Richard sat observing them, then he got up and walked over to the reception desk.

"Yus, sair? Can I help you?" a young clerk asked in a briskly polite tone.

"Can you tell me whether Miss Eileen Snape is staying here?"

The clerk turned and consulted a board out of Richard's sight.

"Yus, sair. Room 264. Perhaps you would like to call her on the house telephone." He gestured imperiously. "Over thaire."

"Thank you. I'll do that."

Richard went across to the row of phones and asked for room 264. It occasioned him no surprise when there was no answer. When the girl on the telephone offered to have Miss Snape paged for him, he thanked her, but told her not to trouble.

He moved over to the other side of the lobby where a pleasant-faced young man in the hotel's dove-grey livery was standing doing nothing.

"Excuse me, but do you know Miss Snape by sight? I believe she's been staying here about a couple of weeks."

The young man nodded amiably. "Miss Snape is lady in lounge with gentleman."

"I thought it was," Richard murmured with a grateful smile. "But I didn't want to make a fool of myself by going up to the wrong person."

The young man beamed uncomprehendingly, a beam which froze into embarrassment as Richard took a coin from his pocket. Luckily, Richard noticed the look in time and muttered something about buying a paper at the bookstall, and the young man's expression relaxed. That was something else the western world had not accustomed him to, people refusing tips and actually going into preliminary agonies before they were proffered.

He had now found out all he wanted and decided he'd better get out before he was confronted by Caspar in the lobby.

In the taxi on the way back to his own hotel, it came to him with sudden alarm that Caspar might be staying there too! An inquiry at the reception desk soon sat his mind at rest, however. With great regret, the clerk informed him that no Mr. Caspar was registered as a guest of the hotel. He was so sorry. Richard forebore to point out that he wasn't.

He decided on the spur of the moment to go in search of Miss Shima. Even if he didn't find her, it would be pleasant to spend the evening midst the bright lights and conflicting aromas of Shinjuku.

A taxi set him down at Shinjuku Station and this time he found his way to the Tanacho Bar without any difficulty. There was still the ill-lit interior, the strident canned music and the girls in golden lamé.

To the one who came forward to conduct him to a table, he said, "Is Miss Shima here tonight?"

"Mishima, Mishima," she repeated with a giggle.

"Miss Shima," he articulated carefully.

"You like beer?" she countered.

"Yes, I like beer," he said with a sigh. He'd wait till he'd been served and then try with another girl.

"I fetch you beer."

"Fine."

She frowned. "You not want beer?"

"Yes, I do want beer."

"I fetch beer."

He gave her a vigorous nod and she departed. A few seconds later, he saw Miss Shima come through the door at the back and go and stand with two other girls by a service table. The place was virtually empty, and its golden gowned attendants were grouped around in postures of polite boredom.

He rose and began walking across to her. She turned her head at his approach and her face registered almost comical surprise.

"Mr. Monk!" she said disbelievingly.

Without further word she followed him back to his table.

"I had to come back to Tokyo on sudden business," he explained, "and I thought I would come and see if you were still here."

She smiled her rather sad little smile. "You see, I am still here." She paused before adding diffidently, "You have things to tell me?"

"Yes," he said gravely. "You remember telling me that your brother disappeared soon after his return from England and that you later heard that he was dead?"

"Yes, I tell you that."

"Well, my information is that your brother was killed on the orders of this man Caspar. I have no evidence—you understand what I mean by that?—but I believe that that is what happened. I'm afraid it's not very happy news; on the other hand it's more or less what you thought had happened."

"You have found this out all for me?" she asked, her eyes shining.

It seemed less unkind to accept the coming, if undeserved, accolade than to reject it with a churlish explanation that he'd come across the information by accident.

"It's not very much, I'm afraid, but I'm glad, at least, to be able to give it to you in person."

"You are very kind man, Mr. Monk. What can I do for you in return?"

"Nothing."

"And this man Caspar, who is so bad. He will go to prison, yes?"

A distant, thoughtful expression came over Richard's face. Then putting a sympathetic hand on Miss Shima's, he said, "I think it's a very strong possibility."

The next morning a few minutes after nine o'clock, Richard put through a call to the other hotel.

"I wish to speak to Miss Snape in room 264," he said with a tingle of excitement. Then: "Is that Miss Snape?"

"Yes. Who is that?"

Richard took a deep breath. "Just before I answer that question, Miss Snape, is anyone listening in to our conversation?"

"There's no one in my bedroom, if that's what you mean. I can't answer for any eavesdroppers along the line."

"I'll have to risk that. My name is Monk, Richard Monk. I'm a London solicitor. I'd like to see you privately about a matter of great urgency."

"Can't you give me some idea what it's about?"

"It's about a Mr. Caspar . . ."

"Am I meant to know someone of that name?"

"Yes, you are, Miss Snape. In fact you were talking to him in your hotel lounge yesterday evening."

There was a pause. "You said just now that you were a solicitor, Mr. Monk. May I ask whose interests you represent in this particular matter?"

"Not Mr. Caspar's."

"Monk," Richard heard her murmur in an apparent aside.

"Is there someone with you?" he asked anxiously.

"No, I've told you there's no one here. I was just trying to recall where I've heard that name before."

"Perhaps Mr. Caspar mentioned it?"

"No, it wasn't he . . . Yes, I remember . . . I know who you are, Mr. Monk. I've seen your name in the newspapers recently."

"Could be."

"And what has brought you all the way to Tokyo?"

"That's something I'll tell you when we meet."

"*When* we meet!"

"I suspect you might find a meeting as useful as I hope to."

"It's possible."

"If it's convenient, I'd like to meet you this morning. Not at either of our hotels, but somewhere inconspicuous. There's a bar called George's Place in Sotobori-Dori Avenue. Could we meet there at half past eleven?"

139

"I don't see why not, Mr. Monk."

"By the way, it's vitally important that Mr. Caspar doesn't find out about our meeting. I don't want him to know that I'm in Tokyo."

"I can imagine that," she remarked dryly.

"Is he staying at your hotel?"

"No."

"Can you get away without being observed?"

"So you think I'm being kept under observation?"

"Don't you?"

"I know I am, Mr. Monk, but for a rather different reason than you probably suppose . . . However, don't start questioning me about that now. I think you can leave it to me to get out of this Japanese honeycomb without being followed. It won't be the first time . . . See you at half past eleven then, Mr. Monk."

23

The sense of euphoric unreality which had encompassed Richard on his outward journey claimed him again on his return flight. But on this occasion it was less euphoric and more unreal. Seen in retrospect his three days in Tokyo had been a succession of electric shocks; Caspar's presence in the city had been the first—Richard had later gone through nail-biting anxiety in his efforts to make sure they didn't fly back on the same plane—and his meeting with Miss Snape had provided the others.

Looking back now, as the plane once more flew over the seemingly endless vista of snow which covered mother earth like a white skull cap, he felt exultant, yet a little frightened; excited yet full of dread. He had uncovered something which he understood only in part and, because of this, he'd been made to feel suddenly afraid. Afraid of something which fell right outside the range of his own experience: further afraid because he was deliberately exploiting that something. He was like a man driving a super-charged Alfa Romeo when he'd previously only driven a low horse-powered family saloon. It looked as though he might yet get in past the winning post without disaster, but only time would tell . . .

"I haven't cooked you any breakfast, Mr. Monk, seeing how you felt last time." It was good to be inside his own flat again and be brought very much back to reality by the practical Mrs. Fleet. "But I'm doing a shepherd's pie for your lunch," she went on, "with a jam tart to follow;"

He nodded weakly. "Sounds lovely, Mrs. Fleet."

"Mr. Scarby and that Miss Wyatt both phoned not more than half an hour ago." When anyone didn't meet with Mrs. Fleet's approval, mention of their name was prefaced with "that". Sarah had been in this category since sending him flowers on his last return from Japan.

"Thanks, Mrs. Fleet. I'll call them both later. Right now I'm going to have a shower."

"Planes are dirty things, aren't they?" observed Mrs. Fleet, who had never been closer to one than seeing them fly overhead.

He phoned Alan in Chambers. "When can we meet? I'd prefer not to talk over the phone."

"Successful?"

"Yes."

"That's all I wanted to know," Alan said with a rare note of excitement in his voice. "We can meet when and wherever you wish. Come along to Chambers, if you like. I'm in all day. Or I don't mind coming along and sharing your lunch if Mrs. Fleet won't glare at me."

"That's a good idea, Alan. I'll expect you about one."

Afterwards, he telephoned Sarah at her flower boutique.

"I'm back," he announced cheerfully. "I understand you called."

"I wonder Mrs. Fleet troubled to tell you. I don't think she likes me. She feels I'm trying to snatch you away from her."

Richard gave a tolerant laugh. "You women!"

"If that's meant to be referring to Mrs. Fleet and myself, I'd be happier if you didn't lump us together."

"Why not?"

"I just would."

Richard sighed. This was an idiotic conversation and, moreover, Sarah was becoming more prickly by the minute. It was odd the way some conversations took a wrong turn early on and never regained their intended path.

"When am I going to see you?" he asked in a placating tone.

"That's up to you."

"Come in for a drink this evening."

"Sure?"

"Of course I'm sure. I wouldn't suggest it if I wasn't."

"How was your trip?" she asked in a meek voice.

"Successful, I think."

"You never really told me why you had to go?"

"You needn't worry, I didn't tell Mrs. Fleet either."

It was after four o'clock when Alan left to return to Chambers, by which time he and Richard had firmly charted the course of Eddie Butcher's defence.

Each of them felt a tingling nervousness as they made a final review of the proposed line of action.

"Final, but not irrevocable," Richard observed cautiously as he stood talking to Alan at the front door.

"Nothing's ever irrevocable until you actually open your mouth in court," Alan conceded. "But I don't see our having any change of heart about this, do you?"

"No, I don't."

"Good. There's just one thing to remember. The only precaution to take when playing with dynamite is to avoid blowing yourself up. And there isn't any doubt that we shall be handling dynamite. Great, sweaty lumps of it."

24

Eddie gazed at the scene around him with an expression of bemused interest, unaware that he himself was also attracting a good deal of attention.

He had, a few seconds before, been brought into court from the cells below, which had smelt strongly of damp disinfectant, and was standing at the front of the dock with a prison officer on either side of him. They weren't a bad couple; on the other hand, during the time he'd known them neither had inspired him with any desire for friendship. Anyway, he couldn't credit any normal-minded person with wanting to be a prison officer.

He glanced first at the judge, whose name Richard had told him was Mr. Justice Grant. There were two judges sitting at the Assizes and Richard had mentioned that this was the junior one who had the reputation for being something of a judicial whizz kid. The senior one was less flexible and more traditional in his approach to trying cases. He was also slightly deaf and less quick off the mark than his younger colleague. He was also considerably milder in his punishments, not that that was a factor in a murder trial where conviction carried a fixed penalty.

As far as Eddie's case was concerned, Richard had added, there probably wasn't anything to choose between them, though it was known that Mr. Justice Grant thought well of Alan.

At this moment the judge was sitting back in a relaxed manner as though he himself was waiting for something interesting to happen. His wig looked crisply fresh and his scarlet robe similarly proclaimed his recent elevation to the Bench. He wasn't wearing a hearing aid—he didn't even have on spectacles. Indeed, he looked positively youthful, to Eddie's considerable surprise. He hadn't thought that anyone became a judge before most people's retiring age.

In the well of the court which separated the bench from the dock sat counsel and solicitors. Richard and Alan were to Eddie's right, one in front of the other. Alan gave Eddie a small smile as their eyes happened to meet. He also wore a comforting air of relaxed calm. Richard was burrowing through a mound of papers like a dog digging for a bone.

The jury was now being empanelled by the clerk and Eddie turned his head in their direction. They could have scarcely looked a more ordinary bunch of people. He didn't find it particularly reassuring to think that his fate hung upon their collective view of what transpired in court over the next few days. He knew, however, that Richard and Alan had scrutinised the list of jurors in advance and made such inquiries as they could to ensure that none of Caspar's friends slipped on. However, as Richard had pointed out, it was much easier to nobble a jury so that an acquittal or a disagreement ensued, than to bring about a conviction by undue methods. Nevertheless, Caspar's writ running as allegedly far as it did, no chances were being taken.

He craned his head round to see who was in the public gallery and found himself looking straight at Tendo and Ebony, whose eyes were riveted on him like four pistol barrels. For five seconds he returned their unwavering stare, then flicked his gaze on.

Ralph Caspar and the other witnesses would be somewhere out of court. And even further out of sight was Diane, awaiting Richard's summons to get in a car and come.

Thought of Diane caused Eddie to swallow suddenly. She, more than anyone, had helped him to get through these past few weeks. He felt an overwhelming gratitude to the fates which had brought him back across the world, and her rallying to his side. Even if he were to be convicted—wickedly and wrongly convicted—he'd still be glad that he'd returned. He could now face any future with her help and, at this moment, he felt ready to make any sacrifice to keep her love. He didn't believe that even twenty years in prison would change that . . . He didn't dare contemplate it . . .

One of the prison officers plucked at his sleeve, bringing him back to reality. The Clerk of Assize was addressing him.

"Edmund Stephen Butcher, you stand indicted with murder, the particulars being that on the seventeenth of April this year, in this county, you murdered Paula Caspar. Do you plead guilty or not guilty to that indictment?"

"Not guilty."

His mind drifted away again as the clerk began to swear the jury. Why did it all have to be so protracted and ponderous! He wished they'd get on with trying him. Would the proceedings proper never start!

They did, however, a few minutes later when Mr. Hetherington Q.C., who was leading for the Crown, rose to address the jury.

Eddie listened as prosecuting counsel explained what evidence he would be calling to prove the charge and then went through it in exhaustive detail. The jury listened to him in hypnotised silence, though one or two had begun to squirm before the end. Their seats were on the hard side and Mr. Hetherington's delivery did little to mitigate their physical discomfort. Moreover, most of them hadn't had to sit still and concentrate like this since leaving school and they were out of practice.

"So, as you will see, members of the jury," Mr. Hetherington was now saying. "There are two main pillars of evidence in the case put forward by the prosecution. One is the evidence of Mr. Caspar, which I have outlined to you, the other is the evidence contained in the signed statement made under caution by the accused. Put those two together and, in the submission of the prosecution, there is only one inference which emerges. Namely, that this man"—he pointed an eloquent finger in Eddie's direction—"murdered Mrs. Caspar."

"There is one further matter which I ought to mention to you before, with the assistance of my learned friend, I start calling the evidence. It concerns motive." He spoke the word as though it were a dread disease. "It is not, of course, incumbent upon the prosecution to prove a motive in this case. Sometimes motives are obvious, at other times not. Now this is a case which has attracted a great deal of public notice. You may even have read things about the alleged background of some of the people connected with it." Mr. Hetherington gave the jury an admonitory shake of his head. "Put such matters right out of your mind, members of the jury. You may be tempted to speculate—it's that sort of case—but don't. Fasten your attention on to the evidence and listen carefully to what my lord says to you about the law and reach your verdict according to those considerations and none other. Remember that every witness is entitled to have his evidence weighed by you with equal impartiality. Leave aside all prejudice, forget anything you may have heard about persons concerned in this case and return a true verdict according to the evidence given in *this* court."

"And long live the Queen as well," Alan murmured to

Richard as Mr. Hetherington sat down. "I wonder if the jury got the point that all the business about their having possibly read things about persons connected with the case was meant to be telling them that Caspar was as good as any other witness, and that though the whole country knows he's nothing other than a superior sort of gangster he still knows how to tell the simple truth his mother taught him."

Richard grinned. "He certainly wraps it up."

"The trouble is you've only got wrappings at the end. Whatever was inside has become lost."

The first three prosecution witnesses were all formal and their evidence was quickly heard. No one in court could have been unaware of the growing electric tension which reached its climax when Mr. Hetherington announced, "I now call Ralph Caspar."

Everyone's head turned toward the door at the back of the court through which Caspar now came. Only a dramatically focused spotlight was lacking. He was wearing a dark blue suit with a white shirt and a black tie. His iron-grey hair was neatly groomed as if he had come straight from the barber's chair.

Alan watched him with quizzical interest as he took the oath in a just right tone of voice. He neither mumbled it incoherently nor did he roar it out in the stentorian tones of the type of witness who takes the first opportunity to ask that he shall be struck dead if he's not telling the truth. And he couldn't be better dressed for the public role of bereaved husband either. Black tie on a white shirt was a perfect touch.

"Your name is Ralph Caspar?" Mr. Hetherington asked in a tone which tried to convey that this was just another witness on the endless conveyor belt of justice.

"It is."

"And you are a company director?"

"That is correct."

"Do you know the accused man, Butcher?"

Slowly Caspar turned his head and gazed without a flicker of emotion at Eddie. It seemed to those watching that he stared at him for an inordinate time before slowly looking back at prosecuting counsel.

"Yes, I do."

"How did you come to know him?"

"Through business. He worked for me at one time."

"Yes, I don't think we need go into any details of that," Mr. Hetherington said and quickly turned a page of his brief.

"But wait till Scarby starts to cross-examine on it," one reporter whispered to another with relish. "The fur will fly then all right. I hear the defence are really going to rip Caspar wide open."

"How long have you known him?" prosecuting counsel now asked.

"Between two and three years."

"Now, shortly before your wife's death, did you receive a phone call from the accused?"

"I did."

"When was that?"

"The day before my wife was murdered. It would have been the Thursday."

"What did he say?"

"He said he wished to see me urgently. He'd been abroad for two months and had just got back."

"Did he say what he wished to see you about?"

"No, he was rather mysterious about it. He said he was very anxious that our meeting should be kept secret and he asked if I could suggest something."

Eddie glanced scornfully across at the witness. If he hadn't had it drummed into him by Richard that scenes in court invariably boomeranged against the person creating them, he'd have expressed his view of Caspar's veracity with matching eloquence.

"And did you suggest something?"

"Yes, I told him that if he cared to come down to 'Woodlands'— that's my house in the country—the next evening, I'd be there and he could tell me what it was all about."

"Did you make any other suggestions about the meeting?"

Caspar nodded slightly. "Yes, I did. In view of his request for complete secrecy, I suggested that he should come to the french window of my study and that I would let him in. I said, that way not even my wife, if she happened to be in, would know of his visit."

"What time was he to come?"

"Half past ten."

"On the Friday night?"

"Yes."

"Well, what in fact happened, Mr. Caspar?"

"About seven o'clock that evening, I was called up to London to an urgent meeting . . ."

"Just let me interpose and ask you something about this

meeting. Where was it held?"

"At my flat off Baker Street."

"And who else was present?"

"Mr. Haymore Jarvis, my solicitor, and Mr. Pyxford, my accountant."

"Yes, the police have taken statements from those two gentlemen," Mr. Hetherington murmured for all to hear.

Alan sprang to his feet. "I must protest my lord, if my learned friend is purporting to give evidence. In any event, it was a most improper observation coming from counsel. It was clearly intended to convey to the jury that these two gentlemen clearly intended to convey that this meeting took place."

The judge nodded. "What *was* the purpose of your comment, Mr. Hetherington?"

"My lord, I certainly didn't seek to do anything improper. I was, to be perfectly frank, merely thinking aloud."

"That's a very dangerous practice in court, Mr. Hetherington," the judge replied severely. "Please let your thoughts remain unexpressed until you are sure that they may be properly expressed." He turned to the jury. "Members of the jury, so far as you and I are concerned, the point has been reached in the evidence where the witness attended a meeting at his flat in London at which, he tells us, a Mr. Jarvis and a Mr. Pyxford were present. We have yet to learn whether or not there is any dispute as to the circumstances of that meeting. I direct you to put out of your minds Mr. Hetherington's rather unfortunate piece of thinking aloud." He gave them a small knowing smile, which seemed to say, "counsel will be counsel" and turned back to Mr. Hetherington who was far too experienced and wily an operator to have been put seriously out of countenance by the rebuke, which he had, in any event, courted as a calculated risk.

"And how long did this meeting last, Mr. Caspar?"

"Until just before eleven o'clock."

"Had you put off the accused's visit?"

"No."

"Why not?"

"I didn't know how to get in touch with him. He'd refused to tell me where he was staying when we'd spoken on the phone."

"So what did you do?"

"I asked my wife to ..."

Mr. Hetherington held up a cautionary hand like a constable

on point duty. "You mustn't tell us what you said to your wife, but you explained the position to her, is that it?"

"Yes."

"And what did you do after your meeting had finished?"

"Drove home."

"What time did you arrive?"

"About midnight."

"And what did you find?"

Caspar hung his head for a second. "I found my wife dead, shot through the back of the head."

"Was she sitting as shown in the fourth photograph of the album, exhibit 1?"

"Yes."

Mr. Hetherington bent down and held a brief, whispered conversation with his junior.

"Did the accused know your wife?" he asked, looking up.

"He'd met her a number of times."

"And just one final question—a purely formal matter—did you identify the body of your wife to Detective-Inspector Drew?"

"Yes."

"Thank you, Mr. Caspar," Mr. Hetherington said in a tone of dismissal and sat down.

The air of expectancy, as Alan rose to cross-examine, was like that which prevails before the sulphurous hiss and splitting crash of a thunderstorm directly overhead.

The reporters lent forward like a well-drilled ballet determined not to miss a nuance. At Alan's first question, they frowned slightly. This wasn't thunder. It was scarcely a plop of rain.

"Is all you've told the court the truth?" he asked, with his head slightly on one side as if to ensure he caught the answer correctly.

"It is," Caspar replied impassively.

"Do you know a Miss Snape—a Miss Eileen Snape?"

It was several seconds before Caspar replied. During this time he simply stared at Alan as though trying to read his mind, while the reporters felt their noses twitching without knowing why. Instinct, flair, whatever you choose to call it, told them to stay on the edges of their seats.

"Yes, I do know a Miss Snape," Caspar replied evenly.

"Who is she?"

"My sister-in-law. That is, my wife's sister."

"She lives at 'Woodlands', your country house, doesn't she?"

"Yes. She acts as housekeeper."

"Where is she now?"

"Abroad."

"Where abroad?"

"She went to Spain on holiday."

"When?"

"The day before my wife's death."

"Have you seen her since then?"

"No."

"Been in touch with her?"

"I've had a couple of postcards without addresses."

"Where was the last one from?"

"I can't remember."

The reporters became restive. What was Scarby asking all these questions about Caspar's sister-in-law for? Why didn't he land a few punches on Caspar himself! Anyone could see that these questions were childish in their lack of effect.

"How long a holiday does Miss Snape usually take?" Alan inquired, to their further bewildered disgust.

"It's up to her."

"She's been away all of six weeks?"

"I understand that civil servants get six weeks' holiday . . ."

"I see, so you don't find anything unusual in her being away so long?"

"Nothing at all."

"Is it possible that she's in Japan?"

Caspar, who had been standing in a relaxed manner, stiffened, and with one hand grasped the side of the witness box as though it had suddenly tilted.

"I suppose she could be," he said, his tone for the first time betraying signs of nervousness.

"I put it to you, Mr. Caspar, that you met Miss Snape in Tokyo twelve days ago?"

Mr. Hetherington and the judge both looked sharply toward the witness, who stuck out his lower lip in apparent contemplation of the question.

It seemed an age before he answered, then he said slowly, "I think, Mr. Scarby, that somebody has seriously misled you."

To the audible astonishment of the Press and even the visible surprise of Mr. Justice Grant, Alan said, "So be it. That's all I have to ask this witness." And he sat down.

25

"What the hell's he playing at?" a reporter asked his companion as they returned to court after the luncheon adjournment. "Either he's gone clean off his head or he thinks he's got an ace tucked away somewhere."

"He'll need a whole pack of aces, the way the trial's going at the moment," his companion replied. For Alan had failed to cross-examine any of the succeeding prosecution witnesses, and Detective-Inspector Drew was the only one who remained to be called.

Mr. Justice Grant had been as surprised as anyone, but had kept his own judicial counsel and made no attempt either to question Alan's handling of the case or to indicate in any way his growing perturbation. Alan Scarby was an able and experienced young counsel who presumably knew what he was up to. Until there were signs that he had taken complete leave of his senses, the judge didn't consider it part of his duty to interfere, despite how he felt about the way the case for the defence was being conducted.

Inspector Drew stepped into the witness-box after the adjournment with the air of a marathon runner agreeably surprised to find he has finished the course after all, but yet with the niggling doubt that he may have got caught up in a different race somewhere along the way.

He described the scene he found at 'Woodlands' on the fateful Friday night and answered a large number of detailed questions from Mr. Hetherington about the lay-out of the room and the position of various objects. Finally, he went on to give evidence of his interview with the accused, who had voluntarily come to the police station with his solicitor, and he produced the written statement under caution which Eddie had signed before being charged.

"Yes, Mr. Scarby?" the judge inquired, almost hopefully, when Mr. Hetherington sat down.

"I have only one question to ask the witness, my lord," Alan said. "Inspector Drew, can you point to any detail in my

152

client's statement which your inquiries have shown to be untrue?"

"No, sir."

"I'm much obliged," Alan said resuming his seat.

The judge sighed a trifle unhappily. Then turning to the witness, he said, "I have one or two questions to put to you, Inspector. I see from the pathologist's evidence that Mrs. Caspar was five feet four inches tall. Assuming she was sitting reasonably upright in the chair in which she was found dead, are you able to give the jury a rough idea of how much of her head would appear over the top of the chair as seen from the rear? Do you follow my question?"

"Yes, my lord. I would say that only just the top of the head would appear."

"So that a person entering by the french window mightn't even be able to tell who it was sitting in the chair, only that someone was there?"

"That is so, my lord."

"And as you've already told us, the room was poorly lit?"

"Yes, my lord. There was only light from a table lamp in one corner of the room."

Mr. Justice Grant pursed his lips. He was unaware Caspar had propounded the theory that Eddie had shot his wife in mistake for himself, but it was one which the evidence, plus the apparent lack of motive, had produced in his own mind as a possibility and he had decided to probe it.

"Thank you, Inspector." He looked down at prosecuting counsel. "Is that your case, Mr. Hetherington?"

"Yes, my lord."

"Very well. Now, Mr. Scarby?"

Alan rose, hitched up his gown and fixed the judge with a firm, sane look. At the same moment, Richard hurried unobtrusively out of court.

"My lord, I have a slightly unusual application to make. It is that, with your lordship's indulgence, and the concurrence of my learned friend, I may be permitted to call someone other than the accused as my first witness. The reason for my application will be readily apparent when I call the witness, and I would ask your lordship's further indulgence in not asking me to be more explicit at this moment."

Mr. Justice Grant gave Alan a long-suffering look. Then with a small baffled shrug, he said, "Have you any objection, Mr. Hetherington?"

Prosecuting counsel, who was filled with a certain euphoria on account of the case having gone considerably better than he'd expected, rose to his feet.

"None at all, my lord," he said graciously.

"Members of the jury, I ought to explain to you that it is a rule of practice that the accused in a criminal trial always gives evidence before any of his witnesses, provided of course he desires to give evidence at all. The reason for this is simple, it prevents his evidence becoming in any way coloured by that of his own witnesses. As you will have observed, all witnesses remain out of court until they are called into the box. That being for the same reason, namely that they can't be influenced by what someone else has said. You've heard Mr. Scarby's application to me. He knows the risks and has undoubtedly weighed them. In the circumstances, however, I am prepared to exercise my discretion in his favour and grant his application." He turned back to Alan. "Very well, Mr. Scarby, call your witness."

Alan gave a little bow to the judge, then said in a loud, clear tone, "I call Mrs. Paula Caspar."

26

It seemed to Alan that the door at the back of the court would never open. And all the while he avoided looking in the direction of the judge from whom he expected, at any moment, a judicial thunderbolt. But none came, if only because Mr. Justice Grant had the unaccustomed sensation of being temporarily out of his depth. Eventually the door did open and Paula Caspar entered. Her progress to the witness box could not have stunned those in court more if she'd been the reincarnation of Queen Elizabeth I.

She faltered over the oath, but recovered her composure and faced Alan with an anxious frown.

"Is your name Paula Caspar?" he asked, in a voice which had become suddenly hoarse.

"Yes."

"Do you see your husband in court?"

She glanced around and then pointed a gloved finger at Caspar who was sitting in a dazed and shrunken huddle next to Inspector Drew, said, "Yes, I see him there."

"Mrs. Caspar," Alan said, beginning to feel some of the tension leaving him, "my lord and the jury have heard evidence indicating that you had been murdered. But you are obviously very much alive. Who was killed in your house on the evening of the seventeenth of April?"

"My sister, Eileen."

"That is Miss Snape?"

"Yes."

"Do you know who killed her?"

"I do."

"How do you know?"

"Because I saw it happen."

"And who was it?"

"My husband."

"What did you actually see?"

"I saw him come through the study french-window and shoot her from behind as she sat in the chair."

155

"Where were you?"

"Standing in a corner of the room out of sight."

"And what did you do afterwards?"

"I confronted my husband."

"And what was his reaction?"

She cast a look of cold hatred in his direction, but he was too far sunk into a state of mesmerised dejection to notice it.

"One of extreme shock."

"Was there a discussion between you?"

"There was," she said.

"And what was the upshot?"

"You don't want to know what passed between us?" she queried in surprise.

"I'm afraid it's not admissable evidence."

"Oh. The upshot was that within two hours, I was on a plane to Madrid."

"Under what name?"

"Under my sister's name."

Mr. Justice Grant now removed his attention from the witness and looked at Alan.

"Mr. Scarby, the witness has answered what I might call a number of incriminating questions. I haven't given her the usual warning about possible consequences since it seems to me, as I'm sure it has occurred to you and to Mr. Hetherington, that in fact what she has said in this court cannot possibly be used in evidence against her husband and by that token she cannot therefore in law be incriminating herself."

"I respectfully agree, my lord," Alan said.

"It doesn't seem to me, Mr. Scarby," the judge now went on, "that you need take this any further. Indeed, I think the less said in this court, the better. There is only one matter which I would like to deal with and that is to tender independent proof that this lady is, in fact, Paula Caspar."

"That's not Paula," a voice suddenly called out from the public gallery.

Mr. Justice Grant looked up to where Tony Tendo was leaning over the edge of the gallery and waving his arms about. An embarrassed police officer was glaring at him and bellowing, "Quiet there."

It was Jack Ebony, however, who dealt with the situation. Tugging Tendo back into his seat, he hissed at him angrily, "Shut your mouth, you stupid bastard! Who are you trying to help?"

"I have evidence available, my lord," Alan said, when the disturbance had subsided. "I'll call Mr. Dunbar, her bank manager." In an aside to Richard he murmured, "You can't have anyone more independent or respectable than a bank manager."

After Mr. Dunbar had come and gone, Mr. Justice Grant addressed the jury.

"I have already indicated to counsel, members of the jury, that the less said in this court, after this recent dramatic revelation, the better, and I propose to follow that precept myself. We here are concerned only with whether the accused Edmund Butcher murdered Paula Caspar. I take it that you are quite satisfied he did not, since the lady has appeared before you alive. In those circumstances, I invite you to bring in a formal verdict of not guilty."

A few minutes later, the judge had made a brisk exit from court and a scene reminiscent of Piccadilly Circus on Boat Race night had developed, save that it was not the statue of Eros but Ralph Caspar whom the police surrounded with a protective cordon against a battalion of reporters.

Richard and Alan slipped out of court through the dock and down to the cells.

"Phew!" Alan said as he removed his wig and ran a hand across his ruffled hair. "I wouldn't want to go through that again, but at least we did manage not to blow ourselves up."

"I thought the judge behaved splendidly," Richard said.

"Bloody marvellous he was! God knows what he must have been thinking of me most of the time."

"So this is where you've got to!" a voice said behind them. They turned to find Inspector Drew gazing at them with an expression of deep reproach.

Offering him a cigarette, Alan lit one himself and sat down on a wooden bench, leaning back gratefully against the tiled wall. "Sorry, but my legs have suddenly turned to jelly."

Richard sat down beside him, but Drew remained standing as he continued to look at them as if they were a couple of truants.

"Did you have to do it that way?" he asked. "Couldn't you have come and told me when you discovered that Mrs. Caspar was alive? Wouldn't that have been the proper way of dealing with the situation, instead of this dramatic show in court?"

"You really ought to be rather grateful to us," Alan said. "We've softened Caspar up for you. We've demoralised him and shaken his screws loose. All you have to do now is step in and lift the pieces apart. What's more you've got a ready-made charge to put against him which you wouldn't otherwise have had."

"You mean perjury?"

"Too true, I mean perjury. It's about the simplest case of perjury anyone's ever had to prove."

"But what about the murder? The only evidence against him is his wife and she's not a competent witness."

"You haven't started trying to find any other evidence yet."

"I doubt whether there's any to be found," Drew observed gloomily.

"There's Butcher's for a start."

"Pff!"

"Well, that's your problem, I'm afraid," Alan said. He went on, "But don't you see, it was only by deploying our evidence in this highly dramatic fashion that we could be certain of achieving a clear-cut, decisive verdict for Butcher. And God knows we could have become nastily unstuck as it was. If Mr. Monk had come along to you ten days ago and told you he'd found Mrs. Caspar alive in Tokyo, there'd have been conferences and consultations and all manner of comings and goings. Meanwhile, Caspar would have got wind of it—indeed you'd probably have had to go and see him—and then more than likely he'd have skipped the country, and all the time our wretched chap would have been left sweating it out in prison." He paused, "Remember the Bodkin Adams case, how the defence produced a witness who'd overheard those nurses comparing notes in the railway carriage. Well, in that case they didn't dash off to the police with their information, as they might have done. They called their surprise witness in court and achieved a far greater effect."

"Be all that as it may," Inspector Drew said wearily, "perhaps you'd care to tell me exactly what has been going on behind the scenes?"

"I'm sure Mr. Monk will tell you everything he can," Alan replied, cheerfully.

"It all started with a Mr. Poultney," Richard said. "He was the inquiry agent employed by Mrs. Caspar to find out who her husband was carrying on with. After her supposed death, he got in touch with me and suggested that the defence might be interested in having him continue his inquiries. We were. Then Mr. Poultney received a mysterious letter from Japan which purported to show that someone else was interested in the outcome of his inquiries. Although it was unsigned, it asked that information should be sent to Miss Eileen Snape at a hotel address in Tokyo. There were two interesting things about the letter. One was that the writer clearly knew of Mr, Poultney's inquiries and the other—much more significant— was Mr. Poultney's own certainty that the writing was that of Mrs. Caspar." Richard paused. "Well, if anything was going to be done, it obviously required someone going to Tokyo to investigate, so off I went, and almost the first thing I saw there was Caspar with the lady passing herself off as Miss Snape, who was, in fact, his wife."

"Did you know for certain she was Mrs. Caspar at that time?" Drew asked.

"It was a pretty good inference. But she admitted it when we met the next day."

"How did you manage to persuade her to come back to England and give evidence?"

"It wasn't too difficult once I'd realised she was prepared to do anything—*anything*—to spite her husband. She'd have paid someone to put out his eyes and then stood by to watch."

"She sounds a nice girl!"

"Well, after all she did know that he'd intended shooting her and framing someone else for the murder. And she had seen him kill her sister. So she had some reason to feel a trifle put out by him!"

"They're worse than the Borgias," Drew observed. "Any-way, what exactly did happen on the night of the murder, according to her?"

"About ten o'clock that evening, her husband told her he was expecting Butcher in about half an hour's time and that he'd be coming to the study french window. But that he was preparing a little trap for him and would like to rehearse it, so would his wife kindly sit in the high-back chair while he went out and came back in through the window pretending to be Butcher. Well, the whole thing sounded a bit too fancy to Paula. Indeed, as she put it to me, it smelt like a whole sewer-ful of rats. However, she pretended to play along with him, but she got her not overbright sister to sit in the chair for her while she stood in a dark corner of the room to see what happened."

"And she saw her husband actually shoot her sister?"

"She was an eye-witness."

"And yet she can't be called to give evidence against him,"

Drew remarked, shaking his head in weary disbelief of the unfairness of the rules of evidence. "Even though she'd like to," he added, giving the knife a further savage turn.

"Yes, it's tough," Alan said sympathetically, "in a case like this one. But whatever you make, or can't make out of the murder, don't forget you've got Caspar on several other bits of toast. It's the end of him. With luck you should be able to topple his whole little empire."

"That's true," Drew said more cheerfully, "except that I'm only concerned in the murder. All his rackets have taken place on other manors."

"Well, be glad for your colleagues then," Alan said with a grin.

Drew shook his head wearily again. He was like someone who finds two hundredweight of best manure deposited on his front path, instead of in the back garden, and is faced with having to remove it.

Turning back to Richard, he said, "What happened after the murder?"

"A short, intensive period of hard bargaining ensued, I gather; though actually Caspar didn't have much to bargain with. His wife agreed to clear out immediately and disappear in consideration for a cash sum. She didn't tell me how much, but I think one can assume it was sizeable. And he was left to go through with the charade he'd arranged, except that it was his sister-in-law and not his wife who was dead. Luckily for him, her face was badly damaged by the exit wound and, in any event, there wasn't anyone to query his identification of her. So he must still have hoped he'd be able to frame Butcher, though for a different murder from that he'd intended."

"Did Mrs. Casper suggest any motive he might have had for wanting to kill her?" Drew inquired with interest.

"She thinks he'd got on to the fact that he was being watched."

"I don't call that much of a motive for murdering your wife."

"It depends on what's going to be brought to light," Richard said. "If it's something which could threaten your existence, then murder presents itself as a prophylactic. Actually, it wasn't till yesterday that the final bit of the puzzle was handed to me—by Mr. Poultney. He'd discovered who the 'other' woman was. Bridget Tendo, Tony Tendo's wife."

"Mmmm!" Drew exclaimed. "Yes, I do see now. If that had got out, there certainly would have been an earthquake in the

Caspar empire. Tony Tendo may be stupid, but, from all I hear, he treats his wife like she's a prize Persian cat. Feeds her with cream and caviar."

"And think of the use which Paula Caspar could have made of the information!"

"I'm thinking! I suppose Caspar hurried out to Tokyo because Paula was turning the screw a bit tighter?"

"I got that impression. It obviously wasn't something she wanted to discuss in detail with me."

"That's understandable," Drew said blandly. "I imagine even the Paula Caspars hesitate to admit to blackmailing their husbands—even when they're like Ralph Caspar." He glanced at his watch and cocked an ear toward the upper region. "Probably all right to get out now without being lynched by the Press."

"In the course of clearing up the mess we've left on your doorstep, there is one person you ought to take a statement from, whom I've not mentioned."

"Who's that?"

"Diane Paisley."

"Butcher's girl-friend?"

"Yes."

"O.K. Mr. Monk, I'll remember that." He turned to go. "You're a couple of lucky so-and -so's. Your work's finished on this case. Mine's just starting—for the second time round." He reached the bottom of the stairs and paused. "Incidentally, it's a pity you didn't force the issue and make the prosecution call Jarvis and Pyxford."

"Why's that?"

"Because then I could have done *them* for perjury too."

A few minutes later, Alan and Richard made their way back through the now empty court. But not quite empty. Sitting alone in a corner was Eddie Butcher.

"I was told I couldn't miss you if I waited there," he said, holding out his hand and shaking first Alan's, then Richard's. "Thank you both from the bottom of my heart." He picked up the holdall containing his immediate possessions. "Only time will show whether I've learnt my lesson," he said with a twisted smile. "It all depends on whether one person's good sense is enough for two."

"I wonder if they will make it," Richard said in a musing tone after Eddie had gone. "He and Diane Paisley, I mean."

"You've seen her. I haven't."

"I'll give it a fifty-fifty chance."

"Those are not bad odds for a marriage these days," Alan remarked. "Which reminds me, Jane particularly asked me to find out about you and Sarah?"

"Tell her I'll be calling shortly and have her crystal ball well polished."

They parted company in the car park and Richard sat in his for several minutes after Alan had driven off. He had the empty, almost melancholy feeling which the end of a major case always induced in him.

The completion seemed to create a gap in his life, even though there was usually another in the offing.

Perhaps he ought to get married . . . Alan didn't have gaps in *his* life. Then he thought of Eddie and Diane. Then of the Tendos and finally of the Caspars.

He pressed the starter button and reversed out into the centre of the carpark.

He must give it further thought. But careful thought.

>>> If you've enjoyed this book and would like to discover more great vintage crime and thriller titles, as well as the most exciting crime and thriller authors writing today, visit: >>>

The Murder Room
Where Criminal Minds Meet

themurderroom.com